THE UNDYING

JOSEPH ERIC CRAWFORD

Paperback: 978-1-964744-02-5
eBook: 978-1-964744-03-2
Library of Congress Control Number: 2024911438

Ordering Information:

Prime Seven Media
518 Landmann St.
Tomah City, WI 54660

Printed in the United States of America

Sheila Barton was no stranger to the weird and unusual; it was practically where she lived.

The attractive thirty-something reporter sat studying the pile of papers on her desk. Some of which were police reports; others were excerpts from newspaper articles dating back to the early 1900's, while others still seemed to be psychological profiles on several different types of illnesses: everything from schizophrenia to lycanthropy. Sheila went over every inch of every file and report, trying to find someway to make sense of everything that had been coming into the newsroom over the last few days. The headline of one paper read in big, bold letters:

SAVAGE ANIMAL ATTACKS KILL SEVERAL IN HOON COUNTY.

Sheila read the story below for probably the hundredth time---and it still made her blood curl.

Several people had been attacked and brutally mauled by what the authorities assumed to be a wild animal, perhaps a rabid wolf; or possibly a vicious panther. The area in which these attacks happened was a small town named Merced, about seven hours ride outside of the city.

As Sheila sat at her overly-cluttered desk reading, she had to stifle an involuntary urge to shudder.

Get it together, Barton, she told herself. This is what you live for.

Being an investigative reporter for the People's Gazette had always been Sheila's passion. Well, not for the People's Gazette in particular, just any large metropolitan newspaper. As long as the stories were good and the work semi-dangerous, she was quite happy. Now, sometimes though, Sheila had to admit that maybe she'd be better off in another line of work.

The intelligent, yet headstrong, reporter laughed to herself at this thought. She knew deep down that she would never be happy doing anything in her life but chasing down leads for a great story.

To get the truth out to the unsuspecting populace, so everyone would know as she did… there were many unexplained happenings in this world; such as those brutal animal attacks in the small town of Merced in Hoon County.

Sheila lit up a cigarette as she thought back to her first encounter with the "weird' or out-of-the-ordinary.

She had been no more than ten years old, maybe younger, playing in the back yard of her parents' country home. Sheila had no real friends growing up, so the little girl with an extremely vivid imagination made up a few and pretended that they were her "real" friends.

However, one summer afternoon as she sat by the little creek behind their house, just simply playing with all her imaginary friends, the same thing she had been doing for months on end, something extraordinary happened.

Young Sheila felt no different that day, she let her imagination run wild; but that **day** had been different, *very* different. And now, years later, the mature Sheila Barton made a point to never let herself forget just how unusual that day would become…

Lost in her own little make-believe world, tiny Sheila Barton had had a strange encounter with someone or some*thing* of unknown origin.

A long shadow cast upon her as she sat by the creek; it was shaped like a man but there was an element about it was strange; even in her child mind, 10-year-old Sheila knew instinctively it was **not** quite human. At present, the adult Sheila could never remember why the man was scary, but she remembered--- a feeling in her gut-

-- that the thing had been far from normal. She had the vaguest memory of the shape, it seemed to have no face, but it did have two eyes that seemed to glow of their own light; a glow that she would still see in her nightmares, over two decades later.

The figure had stood looking at her for many minutes, not moving an inch near nor away from her. It (or he) just simply looked down, to her ten-year-old perspective, from an incredible height. What Sheila could remember of the figure's body was even more-sketchy in detail; it may have been clad all in black, or perhaps the sun behind its back made the whole shape one big, black blot...

The abrupt sound of her telephone ringing off its hook brought the intrepid reporter back to her current lifetime and she quickly extinguished the cigarette in an over-filled ash tray.

"Sheila Barton," she said, voice slightly raspy from the cigarette. "What can I do for you?"

"Ms. Barton," said the voice on the other end. "I have some news you might be interested in."

The owner of the voice coming from the other end sounded almost muffled, kind of like someone holding a handkerchief over the mouthpiece.

"Who is this?"

"Now, Ms. Barton," chided the muffled voice. "You and I both know that anonymous tipsters never give their names."

Sheila then chided herself for the mistake and went about speaking to her mysterious informant.

"Of course, I apologize."

"Think nothing of it," said the voice, almost cordial. "I know that you've been looking into the recent attacks out in Hoon County. I think I may be of use to you."

"How?" asked Sheila, her curiosity piqued.

"Be at the Break House tonight around 10 o'clock."

"The Break House...?" she knew of the place largely by reputation, a real dive bar, and she was not happy about having to make a trip there.

"Can I expect you? Or should I contact another paper for this information?"

"No!" the reporter yelled, perhaps a little too loudly. Although no one else in the newsroom seemed to take notice, each and every one of them busy with their stories and upcoming deadlines.

"No," she repeated in a softer tone. "You can damn well bet I'll be there."

The informant hung up, leaving Sheila listening to a dead dial tone.

The lady reporter gathered up her purse and car keys, then after grabbing an extra pack of smokes out her top drawer, ran toward the door.

Just as she neared the door marked exit Eggy Quayles, her news editor stepped out his office. As usual his face was beet red!

"And where do you think you're going, Barton?" he asked, his pot belly threatening to burst the last few buttons on his ink-smudged shirt.

"I've got a great lead on those animal attacks."

"Animal attacks?" Quayles gave her a confused look. "What animal attacks?"

Sheila gulped as she tried to think of the proper words to say to her very short-tempered boss. Actually Eggy was one the nicest guys in the place… but she really knew how to piss him off better than anybody.

"Well, Eggy," she began, her throat suddenly dry. "You see, um, I sort of was following up on a story from Hoon County."

"Hoon County…?!" Quayles' eyes nearly popped out his head as he screamed those words.

"Yeah, Eggy, you see…" Sheila said, dancing around the subject. "I've been following a breaking story about a series of deaths by what the authorities have deemed animal attacks in a little town called Merced."

"That's not your beat!" said Eggy, matter-of-factly. "Hell, that's not even in the city!"

Yeah, I know," said Sheila. "But I figured seeing as how it sort of ties into something that happened to me as a little girl…"

Quayles cut the lady reporter off before she could finish. "You're not talking about that time you saw a man with his back to the sun are you?

Not that same shit again!"

"Hey, I can't explain what that was all about. And my parents claim that they never saw a man anywhere near me. Now, that sounds very weird to me. And these so-called animal attack deaths seem to have the same weird vibe to them."

"Oh, so now these animal attacks are 'so-called'? You don't believe the Hoon County Sheriff's Department?"

"I think they're covering something up," Sheila exclaimed. "And I want to know how all this ties in with that strange man; or thing; or whatever the hell it was! I've had the same nightmare for over twenty years, Quayles!"

The news editor backed off a bit when he saw how excited Sheila was getting about the subject.

"Besides," she said, calming down. "I just got an anonymous tip about those attacks."

Sheila almost kicked herself for doing what every smart reporter knew not to--- accidentally giving away such a vital piece of information. A good reporter played things close to the vest; no outside interference was needed, or wanted.

"What kind of tip?" now Quayles' interest in the matter seemed to heighten.

"I can't tell you that, Eggy" she said, knowing he felt the same way as she did. "I just ask that you trust me and let me follow-through on this investigation."

Eggy Quayles stood swaying in the doorway as he thought it over. Sheila longed for a cigarette but knew he was not a smoker, so she just put the craving down, in the deepest pit of her being.

Finally, Quayles came to a decision.

"All right," he said. "But I have a stipulation."

"What's that?" Sheila said, slumping over as if weighed down by a massive force.

"If you are going someplace dangerous," said Quayles, knowing damned well she was. "I want someone to go along with you."

Sheila nearly went through the roof. "Oh, come on, Eggy!"

"That is my one stipulation," he said, unblinking. "Take it or leave it"

"I don't suppose I have a choice, do I?"

"Nope," smiled Eggy, triumphant. The news editor scanned the newsroom for a decent partner for Sheila.

"Now who can I spare?" speaking mostly to himself.

Quayles began walking to the center of the newsroom, leaving the exit now unbarred. Sheila took advantage of this momentary lapse of judgment and ran out of the door.

"Barton!" he screamed. "Barton! Get back here!"

Eggy continued to yell for her, but to no avail, the intrepid (and stubborn) lady reporter was gone.

"When she gets back,' Sheila thought she could hear Quayles say as she stepped on the elevator.

"...She's fired." came the last part of the sentence just as the doors closed.

Oh, great, she said to herself. Now I might be out of a job. But, maybe Eggy would be too busy with managing a very frenetic newsroom to remember. Yeah, thought Sheila, and maybe if frogs had wings---

Chapter **2**

Rider Hague was known throughout the city as an expert in the occult. He had lectured on many circuits and even taught a college class (volunteer elective of course) on the subject.

He'd even earned the honorary title of "Professor" Hague in certain circles.

Hague had always had a fascination with the macabre. He wanted to know as much about what was unknown as possible, to pierce the veil of all that is hidden. Driven by this obsession, he had studied up on the subjects of occultism and arcane mysteries for many years. Hague knew a great deal about alchemy, witchcraft, or Wicca (as true witches called it), and astrology, the study of the stars' and planets' effects on human behavior. He'd studied old folklores about *nosferatu, lycanthropes, daemons, succubae* and *incubi*; in his youth, had read quite a bit about John Dee, that 16th Century scholar who also delved into occult practices like dark magic and divination. Rider Hague knew a lot about the supernatural and the unexplained. That was why he had to tell *somebody* his theory about the newest unexplained mystery in the papers.

Hague had been reading all about the mysterious attacks in Hoon County as well--- in fact, he'd read every article Sheila Barton ever wrote. In his mind, she was the only person other than himself that knew those attacks were **not** from animals of any kind. The occultist had a few theories that he wanted to share with the Sheriff's Department or even local law enforcement. But he feared that they would only call him a crack-pot and lock him up in the loony bin. But he felt that the lady reporter, Barton, would surely listen to him.

She had to!

Hague glanced at his wrist watch, it was almost 10--- and he still didn't know how to explain to Barton that he was the mysterious informant who called her. He went over a hundred scenarios of her possible reaction to this news in his head: ranging from friendly to cool to downright hostile!

But he couldn't back out now, he'd made the call and set up the meet; come hell or high water, he'd have to show some balls for once and follow through on his suspicions. That meant he'd have to face the lady reporter.

As the occultist "professor" became lost in his revelry, he failed to notice the attractive young woman walk in the door of the dive bar.

Sheila Barton felt she was not exactly a beauty but also knew she was far from ugly. Most of the guys in her life called her "cute"; she felt that was an accurate description; and in this place of ill repute crawling with lowly scum, any woman with a pulse was fair game. As soon as she walked in, Sheila was surrounded by burly, unruly men; some longshoremen, some construction workers and some just really, really horny creeps.

"Hey, sweet-cheeks," said one longshoreman, his watch cap barely covering his large head.

"You know what they say about guys with big heads, right?" he leered at her.

But Sheila Barton was anything but helpless. "Yeah, they have brains as small as their peckers."

The group of men burst out laughing, all except the one who'd just been insulted, of course.

"Listen, bitch," said the longshoreman. "I'll snap your neck if it strikes me funny."

"Bitch?" repeated Sheila, unperturbed. "That's the best you can come up with? I call myself a bitch."

Again, the group of men started laughing at the feisty little girl. But the burly longshoreman was no longer playing nice. He reached out with a very large hand and grabbed Sheila by the hair!

The lady reporter kicked him in the shin; then as the big guy bent down to grab his leg, she kneed him the face. Two very solid hits, but neither blow fazed the big man much.

"I like when they fight back," he laughed. "It makes victory all the more sweet."

But before the longshoreman could get any closer, a much larger hand grabbed him by the back of the neck and lifted him off the floor!

The owner of that massive mitt was twice as big as the biggest man there; his face hidden under a hood and most of his gargantuan body covered by a long overcoat. He brought the big man's ear close to his shadow-enshrouded face.

"I believe," said the man-monster. "You owe this little lady an apology."

The stranger's voice was deep and booming, almost demonic in nature. The whole effect was one of great power, but surprisingly, quite a healthy dose of etiquette as well.

The longshoreman croaked out an apology and the man-mountain put him back on the floor as gentle as a lamb. But embarrassment causes people to go against their better judgment and as soon as the man-monster turned away, the longshoreman pulled a knife out of his boot and ran at the hooded stranger.

Sheila screamed in warning, but the knife went in before anyone knew what happened!

Amazingly, the stranger did not react in pain. In fact, the stranger didn't react at all. He merely turned around, in the same motion grabbing the big man's wrists, and with incredible strength crushed both of them in a most disturbing manner.

The longshoreman yelled in pain and fell to his knees, his mangled hands hanging limp on both sides of his burly frame.

Now, the entire bar became deathly silent and for the first time, Rider Hague noticed the lady reporter he wanted to meet.

The patrons in the dive gathered in a large mass staring at the man-mountain who stood motionless in the darkest corner of the bar. One of the drunker fellows suggested that they all attack at once. But the hooded stranger must've read everyone's faces because he spoke with that booming voice again.

"I can take on every person in this dive without breaking a sweat." he warned them. "So, attack if you will. But I ask no quarter and will give none."

Most of the drunks didn't quite understand the elevated vocabulary of the stranger, but Sheila Barton acted as interpreter.

"He means: that if you attack him, he will show no mercy."

The lady reporter then added. "I suggest you gentlemen leave him alone and either go home or get back to your drinking."

"What about Claude?" asked one of the patrons; another longshoreman.

"Claude? Is that Mr. Manners over there lying in a heap with two broken wrists?"

"Yeah," answered yet another.

"Get him to a hospital." Sheila said. "And I wouldn't advise you telling the cops about our big friend here. They got better things to do than get killed."

Three of the longshoremen lifted their unconscious, and badly injured, mate and carried him out of the dive bar.

The man-monster sat down in a dark corner, sipping a much neglected beer as everyone else went back to their drinking and smoking.

Hague observed Sheila Barton as she made an attempt to walk over to the hooded mountain of a person, but the occult professor saw this as his chance and stood in front of her.

"Ms. Barton?" he inquired.

"Listen, pal," she said. "I won't have any trouble kicking your skinny ass."

Hague backed up in shock; then quickly introduced himself.

"I'm Rider Hague. I'm your 'informant'."

After the professor explained to the lady reporter he was her contact, Sheila softened up a bit. But she really wanted to talk to the man-monster who saved her life.

"Um, Mr. Hague," she began. "I want to hear what you have to say. I really do. But I feel I must thank that very, very large gentleman sitting in that very dark corner for saving me."

"Of course, Ms. Barton," stated Hague. "I'll just wait here while you speak to him."

Sheila thanked him and made her way over to the dark corner where her savior quietly sat.

"May I help you?" came the booming voice.

"Yeah, I just want to thank you for saving my life."

"You are most welcome, little lady."

"May I ask your name?"

"You may ask." said the man-monster. "But there is no guarantee that I will give it."

"…Fair enough." remarked Sheila.

The man-mountain motioned for Sheila to sit down at his table. A gesture she gladly accepted.

But as Sheila sat down, she almost seemed to think that she saw the stranger's eyes were glowing.

Either she was mistaken or the stranger moved his head to a different direction, because in the next second she could no longer see the glowing eyes.

And there was always the possibility that she was insane.

Shaking the negativity from her thoughts, the lady reporter settled in for a brief chat.

"What are you drinking?" asked the hooded man.

"Beer…" she said nonchalantly, convinced that she had thankfully been mistaken about the eyes.

"Good choice." said the hooded man, almost sarcastically.

"Whatever's on tap," Sheila clarified. For some reason she found herself really connecting to this large, scary man whose face she had not yet seen and whose name she did not know.

"So," she began. "Your name…?"

"You first…" He retorted.

"All right, we'll play it your way." She said, laughing. "Zelda Lane."

"Really," the hooded man boomed. "Then why did that young man over there, call you Ms. Barton?"

Uh-oh, she'd been caught in a lie. Oh, well, she concluded, no use lying to this man further.

"You're right." she said, smiling. "My name is Sheila. Sheila Barton."

"Nice to know ya, Sheila, Sheila Barton." said the hooded man.

"No, it's just Sheila…" but the lady reporter quickly realized that the man-mountain was only playing around.

"I guess I deserved that." she conceded.

"Well, Sheila, you may call me Adam."

"Adam what…?"

"Just Adam," he said.

"You have no last name?" she inquired.

"Where I come from, Ms. Barton," said the hooded man. "They're not required."

"And where's that? …The Stone Age?" joked Sheila.

Adam laughed at her joke and Sheila realized that he was not going to give her any more information.

Oh, well, she thought, might as well enjoy the company. Of course, there was the little matter of Rider Hague and the inside scoop she was about to get from him.

One beer, Sheila promised herself, and then it's off to learn what I came here for in the first place.

CHAPTER **3**

Rider Hague watched as the lady reporter sat in the dark corner conversing with the extremely large man in the hood and overcoat. His attention was so rapt by them that he did not notice the beauty who placed herself in a chair directly in front of him.

"Hello," said the beauty.

Hague almost fell out of his seat, but quickly recovered from his start.

"Hi," he said, throat suddenly dry.

"Anyone sitting here?" asked the vision of loveliness across from him.

Hague looked at her from top to bottom: the body was magnificent, very shapely; her skin of a light brown tint... bronze like a statue; however, it was her face that made him lose control of his faculties.

Where to begin? He thought to himself. The hair was raven black, and long--- flowing down both sides of her face like a waterfall of darkness.

The woman's face was beyond beautiful, but the eyes!

Her eyes were unlike any he'd ever seen before... an amber gold that seemed to sparkle and shine of their own accord. Hague looked deep into those amazing eyes and found himself getting lightheaded, as if his very soul were soaring miles above the Earth. His entire body seemed to become incorporeal, kind of like those out-of-body experiences he'd read so much about.

"Who are you?" he finally managed to ask.

"I have been called many things in my lifetime." she said aloofly.

"You can't be any older than thirty," he observed. "Maybe even less…"

"How sweet of you to say," said the beauty, still acting evasively. "But I'm much older than you could imagine."

"I know a little about the occult," stated Hague.

"Yes, 'Professor' Hague, I'm very aware of your extended knowledge when it comes to the supernatural."

"Are you a witch?"

"Aren't all women?" she asked with a wink.

"You're not a succubus, are you?"

"What do you think?"

"I don't know anymore," he mumbled. "My head… feels so light …So disoriented right now."

"Of course," she gloated. "Such is my power over the weaker sex."

"You *are* a witch," Hague remarked in accusatory tone.

"That's not entirely what I am, but it's close enough to the truth for you."

Rider Hague tried to remember how to counteract spells of witchcraft, but his mind felt so clouded that he couldn't think of anything but serving the beautiful woman sitting before him.

"I suppose you must call me something …" she said, her eyes shimmering. "…Other than Mistress, of course."

The beauty intensified her gaze and Hague simply stopped moving, entranced.

"You may call me 'Krystyn'." said the beauty. "It's not my real name, but it'll do."

Now, "Krystyn" stood and somewhere inside Rider Hague's clouded brain he heard her voice say to him---

"Rise… my servant."

And he did as he was commanded.

In the darkened corner where Sheila sat talking to the mysterious Adam, a sudden feeling struck the man-monster--- like a beckoning of sorts that he could not explain.

But as soon as Rider Hague rose from the table from which he sat, Adam did the same.

"What's the matter?" asked Sheila.

"I don't know," said Adam, as he walked over to Hague and the raven-haired witch.

"Do I know you from somewhere?" he asked the beautiful woman with Professor Hague.

"I highly doubt one such as you would know someone of my station." said the woman in a haughty manner.

"I feel like we've met before," goaded Adam.

"Listen, beef," she insulted him. "Get away from me or I'll have you executed."

But Adam was not willing to give up so easily and reached for her hand.

Then something amazing happened!

Both his hand and her arm began to steam as soon as they touched one another. Adam and the bronzed beauty screamed out in pain and anger and both quickly pulled away from the other one.

"You cretin!" yelled Krystyn, alerting everyone in the bar, including the befuddled Rider Hague.

"I will have your head for this!"

The hooded man stood holding his still-steaming hand; he hadn't recovered as quickly as the raven-haired witch. While Krystyn, for her part, turned her hypnotic gaze on all the men standing at the bar and in all corners of the dive. Her voice penetrated all their dense skulls and Hague could hear her in his mind as she commanded them to kill the thing in the hood. Unable to resist the voice of their Mistress, every man from 18 to 80 surrounded the hooded man.

"What's going on?" he asked, still somewhat dazed from the painful contact.

Sheila Barton piped up. "We'd better leave, Adam."

Hague made a mental note of the hooded man's name, as much as he could think at moment, that is.

"Why?" asked Adam.

Then all of Adam's questions were answered as the bar patrons attacked en masse. They swarmed him a like a hive of bees; biting, kicking, clawing, punching. Adam fought them all off, but he didn't want to hurt any of them. At least, that's what it looked like to Sheila.

She did what she could to help him, but there were just too many of them and she was nearly trampled. Adam grabbed her up, like a child with his favorite toy, and shoved his way to the door, slapping people aside like they were mere gnats before his mighty fists. Finally, he escaped outside and apparently the mob saw no point in following him.

But as Sheila was being carried away by the extremely large man who saved her life for the second time that night, she remembered Rider Hague and felt a dread deep in her soul for what was to happen to him and all those poor people being terrorized, and slaughtered, in Hoon County.

And being a woman, Sheila Barton knew it was her right to have a good cry. So that's just what she did.

CHAPTER 4

Adam let Sheila down once they were more than block away from the dive bar called the Break House. After her good cry, she jokingly thought to herself they should've just named it the "Dive Bar".

As the lady reporter chuckled at her own private joke, Adam looked at her askance.

"Did I miss something funny?" he asked. "Or were you crying?"

"Oh, no. I never cry," Sheila lied. "I was just laughing at something I was thinking about."

"Ah," said Adam, somewhat distantly.

"No, really," Sheila said, much more self-righteously than she meant to. "I thought it'd be funny if the Break House was called the Dive Bar."

"Why were you there, anyway?"

"I was to meet an informant."

"For what…?" asked Adam inquisitively.

Sheila wondered what business it was of his, but answered anyway. "The guy said he had some information on the animal attacks in Hoon County. The *supposed* animal attacks."

"Oh," said Adam, rather noncommittally. "That story."

"You know about it?"

"I've heard a few things--- 'through the grapevine' as they say."

"Like what?" Sheila eagerly asked.

"Like how each attack took seven victims," he stated.

"How do you know that? I never got that information."

"Cops usually aren't forthcoming with that kind of information."

"Seven each attack?"

"Yes."

"What in hell does that mean?" Sheila asked herself.

"Excuse me?"

"Oh, sorry," she apologized. "I was just thinking out loud."

"Ah."

"Seven people attacked each time." said Sheila, puzzling it out. "These are not random animal attacks. This is some kind of a pattern. These are serial killings."

Adam gazed down at the lady reporter--- well, if his face were not hidden under a hood--- she would've known that he had his attention focused on her.

For the first time Sheila thought about something other than Hoon County, as she stared up into his hidden face.

"Why don't you take off that hood?" Sheila asked.

Adam seemed so shocked by the suggestion, that he actually took a step away from her.

"Because I am not something you want to see," he said finally, with a sadness she could not ignore.

"I've seen many strange things in my life," she assured him.

"You've never seen anything like *me*." he stated.

"Please," she begged. "Let me be the judge of that."

Adam moved his great head upward, as if looking to the sky for guidance or… perhaps God.

"If I show you my face," he began. "It must be in private. Not out on the street like this."

And the big man strode down the street for a destination only he knew.

"Okay." she said, and followed his lead.

Adam led Sheila to a small dilapidated building that had been deemed "condemned" years ago by the city's building inspector and the board of health for multiple violations; not the least of which, Sheila remembered, being its lack of structural integrity.

Each creaking movement made Sheila uneasy; she felt for sure that the entire structure would collapse on them both at any moment. Adam must've noticed her apprehension because he quickly allayed her fears by pointing out that he'd reinforced the structural support by propping up several beams throughout the weakest load-bearing sections.

"I made sure to put metal braces up so nothing could come down on me."

"So, then, we're safe?" asked Sheila, trying to hide her skepticism.

"As safe as can be expected," said Adam. "But I won't keep you here long. I don't think your human system can deal with all the pollutants in this area."

"My 'human system'?" asked Sheila, perplexed by his choice of words. "What does that mean?"

"'There are more things, Horatio…'" he said.

"…on heaven and Earth.'" she finished the quote, slightly.

"So you know some Shakespeare?" asked Adam, sounding impressed.

"I did take journalism in college." she remarked. "Classic literature is something every good writer should learn."

"Then what I have to show you," he said, slowly lowering his hood. "Will make you believe that quote to be absolute truth."

As Adam removed his hood, Sheila stood transfixed. She didn't know whether to scream or faint.

But in any case, her body was not cooperating--- she couldn't open her mouth and her legs wouldn't give out from under her. She merely gaped at the monstrosity that stood revealed before her staring eyes.

"Well, Ms. Barton," said Adam, somewhat coldly. "Happy now…?"

"I…don't…know," she managed to croak out.

Adam, or whatever he really happened to be, appeared inhuman in the most extreme way imaginable. His face was grotesque to the point of being unbearable to behold--- almost indescribable in its ugliness--- but it was his eyes that drew all the attention.

They glowed, greenish in color, like a jack o' lantern on Halloween. As if someone had carved out his orbs and placed two eerie candles behind each socket. Sheila couldn't find words to describe his features. To her, they defied detailed description. All she could think about was the famous monster in Mary Shelley's novel. Adam's skin texture, she noted, appeared somewhat reptilian, almost scaly; but even that didn't seem to be the proper word to use. Sheila reflected on a fact that she'd discovered while researching the occult and pagan religions: some ancient cultures believed that the first proto-humans were of reptilian origin. Was this Adam then the first man-like being?

The biblical Adam even? She was not religious herself, so it was not blasphemy to even think such thoughts. Could he be the true inspiration for all those snake-gods: Quetzalcoatl in the Aztec culture or Dumballa in the Vodun religion?

He wasn't exactly a snake, but he definitely was not a human either.

Sheila became lost in her thoughts; to her mind, Adam resembled nothing she'd ever seen. But there was one aspect of his appearance she could not ignore.

--- Those eyes! She kept coming back to those glowing eyes.

But the lady reporter had to make sure she wasn't hallucinating. A pair of green glowing eyes!

Had this then been the mysterious figure from her childhood? Had he been as large as this monster of a man?

Man? Could she even refer to Adam as a man? And although she wanted to think of him as nothing but a *Thing*--- she couldn't forget how intelligent he was and how gentle he'd thus far been to her.

Finally, Sheila got her voice back.

"Did we ever meet before?" she asked, almost hoping that at last she had found the answer to the one question that had plagued her for most of her life.

"I don't believe so," he said, with not a hint of deception in his booming voice.

"Damn!" she exclaimed.

Now, to Sheila's delight, it was Adam's turn to be stunned. He'd most likely seen other people react to him in all sorts of ways; probably with fear and disgust and hatred. But here she was--- a young woman (not unattractive) who seemed to simply accept him for what he was.

"What's the matter?" he inquired.

"Nothing, I just thought that you were the hooded man I'd seen as a little girl."

"Hooded man?" he asked, seemingly concerned. "Tell me about him."

"Well," began Sheila. "There's not much to tell."

And as Sheila recounted the story of her strange encounter with the mysterious man/thing, Adam seemed to take great interest in her words. "So," he said, noncommittally. "You had a weird episode in your young life that left you craving to know all there is about the unexplained. Is that why you write the stories you do?"

"Yes, I suppose so."

Adam walked to a far corner of his abode and retrieved a handful of newspaper clippings. Sheila realized quickly that they were from her byline.

"Your stories are the only thing in the paper I actually find worthwhile reading."

"Thank you," she said, with a note of confusion. "You read my byline?"

"Indeed I do, Ms. Barton."

"I guess I should be flattered. Not every reporter can say that Frankenstein has read their stories."

"Frankenstein, huh?" asked Adam, with a tinge of sarcasm.

"I'm sorry," apologized Sheila. "I just meant…"

"No, it's fine. I've read the novel… very interesting. But I am not a reanimated amalgamation. I have simply been since the dawn of time."

"That's not possible," Sheila exclaimed.

"My dear young lady," began Adam. "I think I would know a little better than you who I am."

"But how could you be? I mean, how you could hide for so long without ever being…"

"…Seen?" Adam finished her question.

"Yes,"

"I never said that, did I?"

"No, I suppose not. But…"

"Ms. Barton, as I said. This area is not conducive to a human's frail nervous system. You should leave now."

Sheila protested; she wanted to know more about this "Adam".

"All I will say is this: My full name, as it was given me, is--- Adam: The First. That's what it translates into in your modern English, anyway."

And with that, Adam lifted Sheila up in his massive arms and carried her out of the condemned building where he made his home. Before the lady reporter could ask another question, he disappeared back into the dilapidated structure giving one final warning---

"Do not follow me back in here," he commanded. "And good luck with your story."

After Adam's final statement, Sheila listened as the sounds of a major collapse happened inside.

"Adam!" she called out, worried for his safety.

But she received no answer.

"Adam!!" she screamed. "Please answer me!"

No answer, no reply whatsoever came to her waiting ears.

And for the second time that night, Sheila Barton cried.

CHAPTER 5

The phone rang early, too early for Sheila's liking, but she picked it up anyway.

"Hello," she croaked, longing for a cigarette.

"Barton!" yelled the voice on the other end. No need to ask who it was--- she knew that bellow anywhere.

"Morning, Eggy," she said, just trying to test his anger limits.

"Don't 'morning' me, you twit! What the hell happened at the Break House last night?"

Holy shit! Thought Sheila, he knows. But how could he?

"I don't know what you mean," she feigned ignorance.

"Oh, you don't, huh?"

"Nope,"

"Well, then why did I have the commissioner of police call me up and say that one of his patrolmen spotted you going into the Break House at around 10 o'clock last night?"

"Um," think up a good lie she told herself. But it was barely six o'clock. She couldn't think straight until she had that first cigarette.

"I'm waiting for an answer," said Quayles.

"Well, Eggy, you see…" she sputtered. "What I mean is…um…"

"Oh, save it, Barton." he said, fed up. "I want you in my office as soon as you come in."

Great! Now I'm dead-meat, she fumed under her breath.

"You hear me, Barton?" Eggy prodded. "…As soon as you come in."

"Yeah, Eggy, I hear you."

My dead relatives can hear you, she joked.

"Good!"

With that final bellow, Eggy Quayles slammed the phone down so hard Sheila had to pull her ear away from the receiver just to keep from going deaf.

Tight ass! What a bite in the ass! He's an asshole! Sheila couldn't think of anymore words with ass in them so she got out of bed.

She looked at herself in the mirror and did what she figured every small-breasted woman did… she pulled her boobs closer together and pushed them up to give the illusion of having some cleavage.

Sheila laughed at her own self-deprecating joke and went to have her morning cigarette. And a quick shower.

Time to face the firing squad, she thought, for the fourth time-- in just this month alone.

CHAPTER 6

Rider Hague awoke, not knowing where he was or how he gotten there.

The last memory he had was sitting at that dive bar called the Break House, waiting for that woman reporter Sheila Barton. He had information for her that he felt would help her in her investigation of those unexplained animal attacks in Hoon County.

But what happened after that?

Had they hooked up afterward? Did he immediately fall in love with her? He'd seen her picture in a couple of periodicals, but had he been so swept up in lust that he just slept with her?

And why was his head swimming? Had he been drinking as well?

He couldn't hold his liquor worth a damn, so it could be a hangover.

But he was still fully dressed… they couldn't have, if he still---

Oh, man, did his head ever hurt.

"Hello," he called out, softly.

No reply.

A little louder Rider, he told himself. But not too loud: came the mental addendum.

"Hello!" he yelled.

Too loud! His aching head scolded him.

But the greeting was apparently loud enough, because a voice answered.

…A female voice.

"Hi." it said.

"Who are you?" he asked. "Where am I?"

The female voice replied to him in kind. "Which question you want answered first?"

"I don't know. My head is spinning, can't think straight right now."

"Well," said the voice, one he noted, with a country twang. "I'll answer in order of query."

"Fine,"

"My name is Heidi." came the answer to question one.

"Hello, Heidi," Rider greeted her—at least her voice. "I'm…"

"Rider Hague," said Heidi. "I know who you are."

"How?" he asked, full of skepticism.

"That may tie in to the answer to your second question."

"What do you mean?"

"Well," said Heidi. "You are somewhere you may not want to be, but soon--- this will be the only place you'll ever desire."

"I highly doubt that," said Hague.

"Ms. Krystyn is very persuasive," replied Heidi.

Krystyn, he knew that name, where did he know it from? It seemed as if he'd heard the name in a dream; or perhaps a nightmare. In any case, Rider could not place where he'd heard of or met someone named Krystyn.

"Who is Ms. Krystyn?" he said finally.

"I'm hurt that you don't remember me," responded a different female voice.

Now, Rider remembered--- it was her! She was the one whose voice had been in his head last night.

This Kystyn must have used some kind of witchcraft on him and he fell under her spell.

"You…" he began, almost choking on the word.

"You are the woman I met at the Break House."

"You are correct, Mr. Hague," said Krystyn, as she walked into the room.

Once Rider saw her he was immediately reminded why he had not tried to fight her spell harder.

She radiated beauty like an aura; it seemed to envelop her, bathing her entire body in some kind of otherworldly glow. For some inexplicable reason he also found himself standing as soon as she entered.

Her voice; that very persuasive voice was inside his head again--- and he had no will to fight it. And were Rider completely honest with himself, he'd realize he had no *desire* to oppose her commands.

"Who are you?" he asked, trying to sift through the haze that covered his brain.

"I am your Mistress," she said matter-of-factly. "And you are my servant. You and any man I desire to have serve me."

Rider managed to force out one relevant question.

"How… how do you have such power?"

Krystyn laughed at the attempt; then sat down in a chair that seemed to appear from out of nowhere.

"To know my story is to know too much," she said cryptically. "You need only accept that I can make you do whatever I want--- whenever I want."

"But why me…?"

"Because you are very intelligent," she stated. "I have read a few of your papers on the occult. And despite a mistake here and there, your theories are pretty sound."

"Mistakes," he queried. "I made no mistakes, not a one. My research is impeccable. Every detail and factoid strenuously checked and double checked. Not one false fact exists in any of my papers."

"You may see it as so. But I happen to know quite a bit more about the occult than most--- if not all--- people."

The fog covering Hague's mind seemed to be getting denser and as a result his thinking became more and more convoluted. He wanted to ask more questions. Many more. He desired to compose more probing quandaries for this woman to address, but at that moment he could not think of anything at all.

"You have a strong will, Mr. Hague," said Krystyn, sincerely impressed. "But you cannot fight me. Just give in to being my thrall. You will find it quite enjoyable to please me."

Krystyn stood up again, and the chair, seemingly like everything else, which appeared to be under her command, disappeared once its services were no longer needed.

Appearances aside, Rider saw, even in his hazed state of mind, two arms grab the chair and remove it from the room.

So, he thought, not everything she does is connected to the supernatural. Have to keep that in mind, he added.

"Dinner is at seven," said Krystyn as she exited. "Heidi seems to have taken a liking to you. She will watch over you while I'm out."

"Where are you going?" asked Rider.

But no reply came his way.

When he thought himself alone, he collapsed on the bed and stared up at the ceiling. As he focused on the stucco above his head, a face came into his line of sight.

If he had found Krystyn amazing to behold, he was twice as stricken by the angel that now filled his upward gaze.

She was blond and blue-eyed, shapely and pale. Her golden locks were in pigtails that framed both sides of her beautiful face. She wore simple clothing, nothing as extreme as the garish "costumes" Krystyn favored. This one appeared to be a real down-home type.

"Hi," said the angel.

"Hi." came Rider's terse reply.

"I'm Heidi," she said in that twang he'd noted earlier, and extended her pale hand.

Rider took the light-complexioned hand, noted that it was completely hairless and shook it gently.

"Rider," he returned the introduction.

"I know,"

"Oh, that's right." he said bitterly. "You people know all about *me.*"

"Don't be bitter," said Heidi in her light-hearted twang.

"Where you from?" he asked.

"I can't really tell you anything more than what Ms. Krystyn did."

"Surely, telling me where you're from can't hurt anything."

"No, please," she said in an almost begging manner. "I was told to tell you nothing about myself or Ms. Krystyn."

"...Why not?"

"I don't know."

"Then maybe," he began to say, but Heidi backed off violently away from him.

"Don't ask me anymore questions!" she said, in a voice quite unlike her own.

"But, why not...?"

Then Rider thought that for the briefest moment he observed her eyes glow with a yellowish color.

...A very inhuman color.

Rider Hague was wiser than most men and more easily frightened as well--- he knew when to shut up. So that's just what he did.

Heidi appeared normal once more and just as cordial as before.

"You wanna watch the television?" she asked.

"Why not..?" Rider Hague said, for the third time that day.

CHAPTER 7

Sheila Barton sat in her news editor's office, feeling like a little kid being scolded by the school principal. Eggy Quayles had been her boss for the better part of a decade, they'd been real close at one point and now they always felt a bit awkward around each other.

Sheila thought back to the night they'd gone to dinner and she'd finally had the nerve to ask him how the hell he got name like Eggy. Not a nickname or short for Eggbert, his legal name was actually Eggy.

He told her that his father didn't like children and when Eggy's mother told her husband she was pregnant, he reportedly said: "Probably grow up to be a real egg-head."

And that was how the poor bastard got a name like Eggy on his birth certificate and every legal document that ever came down the pike.

Now, Eggy Quayles had the unenviable task of possibly firing his former friend. If nothing else, she was definitely up for censure.

"Sheila," he said, in quite a low tone of voice. "I love your work. There is no one else on staff that goes after a lead like you and follows it through, no matter what."

"But." said Sheila, waiting for the guillotine to come crashing down.

"But...," said Eggy. "I have a certain quota I have to fill. Every now and then, even a serious journalist has to do a puff piece. That's what the readership wants and we have an obligation to fulfill that need."

"Eggy, people are being torn apart over in Hoon County."

"I know," he said, with real regret in his voice.

"Seven a night, Eggy," said Sheila.

"What?"

"…Seven people. In every attack, it was seven people that were mauled to death."

"How do you know that?"

"I met someone last night who gave me that little bit of information. Which apparently the Hoon County Sheriff's Department had conveniently forgot to mention."

"Maybe they're trying to stave off a county-wide panic."

"Or perhaps it's a cover-up for a local serial killer."

"That's a mighty big leap, Sheila." said Eggy.

"Think about it though," she prodded. "Some local boy goes wacko and decides to start hacking up all his neighbors, make it look like a bear or mountain lion on the loose. The Sheriff is told by the county commission to keep all the details secret from the public because they don't want any outside interference… you know, no 'foreigners'."

Quayles looked at Sheila with a mixture of shock and bemusement. She could tell her editor didn't know how to respond to the crazy fairytale he'd just heard.

"Sheila, I called you down here to fire you." he said coldly.

"I know."

"I think I want you to take some time off instead."

Sheila couldn't believe her ears. Eggy was practically giving her his blessing to follow up on her story--- without actually saying those words.

"Really?" she asked, almost beaming.

"Yes."

"So, how long are we talking here? …A couple of days? …Weeks? …Months?

"I don't want to see you again until your mind is right." he said with a slight smile.

"You got it, boss." said Sheila, grinning from ear to ear.

"Why is it you only call me 'boss' when it's convenient for you?"

Sheila didn't answer, she simply grabbed up her purse and kissed Eggy on the cheek.

"Barton!" he bellowed.

Sheila spun around in shock, what had she done? Was it all just a game? Was he fucking with her?

However, one look at Eggy Qauyles' face told her all she needed to know. Time to put on a show.

"And don't come back until I need you! You hear me, Barton?"

"Yeah, I hear you! Thanks for nothing, Quayles!"

Every face in the newsroom was now staring at them both, trying to appear as if they weren't actually interested in the argument going on between superior and subordinate. Sheila fumed as she left the office and headed for the door, her ponytail swaying back and forth as she exited the room.

"What are you all looking at?" screamed Quayles. "You can go right behind her if you want!"

Nobody said a word and Eggy Quayles smiled to himself as he listened to the sound of all the typewriters going simultaneously.

It's good to be the King, he thought to himself. Then remembered the way Sheila Barton had him wrapped around her finger and slumped back into his chair--- deflated.

Sheila finished packing in twenty minutes. The train to Merced in Hoon County would be leaving at noon and she wanted to waste no time in getting there. Eggy's expense account should cover most of what she needed, aside from food that is. But hell, it wasn't as if she had a large appetite anyway.

However, as the investigative reporter thought about the thrill of the hunt, she found herself craving a large double-decker burger and a giant milkshake.

The diner was on the way to the station, she told herself, no harm in being just a little bad.

The train ride to Hoon County was pleasant enough; she had fallen asleep once they were less than ten miles from the city and heading deep into the country.

Sheila always felt more at home in the country. The big city was too crowded and cramped, she felt like it stifled her, making breathing more and more difficult each day.

Hell, if one of these local papers were searching for a good reporter, she might just transplant herself into the country she loved so much. The time displayed on her watch read 5:10. Another hour and she would be in Merced, that small town in the middle of Hoon County and seemingly the epicenter of a serial killer's stalking grounds.

Well, Merced, Sheila Barton was on the case now and she would find out all your dirty little secrets.

CHAPTER 8

Merced was small.

That's the first thing that popped into Sheila's head as she stepped off the train and onto the depot platform. So small, in fact, the lady reporter felt like she had stepped into a scene right out of an old Western.

…She half-expected John Wayne to mosey on up to her and say "Howdy."

The only thing she really noticed in the town, if it could be called that, seemed to be the Sheriff's Office and a boarding house. No other buildings or structures. And, of course, there was the train depot. But that was it.

In the distance she could make a few houses, probably a major farming community in this area.

Maybe she'd run into John Boy, the lady reporter quietly joked to herself.

Taking in a deep breath, Sheila picked up her bags and walked across the road to the boarding house.

The boarding house had apparently once been a prison--- at least it looked that way to Sheila.

The walls were of a drab stone construction and the floor cold, hard concrete. The décor in lobby was very sparse, holding nothing but a table and two chairs. Behind the rotting wooden reception desk, stood a man who looked as if he'd been there when the place was built--- most likely in the early 1800's; maybe even earlier.

Sheila was definitely no expert in historic architecture.

"Morning," said Sheila, as cordially as possible.

"Yep," said the clerk.

"Nice place," she lied to the man's face.

"Yep,"

"Let me guess, you're the chief speechmaker here."

The clerk tilted his head and gave her a sideways gaze, he apparently realized for the first time that an attractive young woman stood before him.

"How can I help you, missy?" he said with a little more enthusiasm.

"I'd like a room."

"…How many nights?"

"At least a week…"

"Sign the register, please." said the clerk as he handed Sheila a ledger that had seemingly been around since Washington's youth.

"You're not going to give me a quill, are you?"

"You're a cute little gal, ain't ya?"

"So I've been told."

"Too bad most of the young fellas left this town a couple years back."

"Is this town part of Hoon County?"

The clerk stiffened at the mention of Hoon County.

"Why?"

"Just curious, is all?"

"…You a reporter?"

"That depends," said Sheila.

"On what…?"

"…On whether or not you like reporters."

"They don't bother me much."

"Good." she said, smiling. "Then I'm a reporter."

"You like that Lois Lane character from the funnies?"

"No… Not really." she answered noncommittally.

"You do know that's fiction, right?" she added.

"Of course I know its fiction. I ain't some dumb hick, ya know."

"Thought never crossed my mind."

If the clerk caught her sarcasm, he didn't bring attention to it. He merely handed her a key and pointed to the stairs behind her.

"It's the first door on your left."

"How many people died in that room?" she asked, still using the sarcasm.

"Too many to name," said the clerk, and Sheila couldn't tell if he was being sincere or ironic.

"Thanks, Shecky," Sheila said as she headed up the stairs.

The room in which she now stood didn't seem to belong in the same building.

It was clean, smelled fresh and even had curtains on the windows. In the corner, barely noticeable upon entry, she noticed a small writing desk and chair situated in front of a small window that overlooked the street. The bathroom, Sheila perceived, was elegant; white porcelain tile and fancy smoked glass shower doors. Even the toilet looked as though it were made for royal asses.

Utterly exhausted by her long trip, Sheila lie down on the bed and immediately felt how soft it was--- she thought to herself, this damned thing is better than my bed!

A sudden knock on the door made her jump up in a start.

"Who's there?"

"It's me, Shecky." said the clerk through the door.

Sheila was really beginning to like this guy; he was a smartass in a way she could handle.

The lady reporter opened the door and noted the clerk stood with clean towels in his hands.

"Thought you might want some fresh linens."

"Thanks." said Sheila, and this time she was sincere.

"The sheriff would like to talk you when you have time." he added as she took the proffered linen.

"Am I in trouble?" she asked.

"No, no, nothing like that a'tall."

"Good."

"Sheriff Monte just likes to meet everyone who comes to Merced."

"Sheriff Monte of Merced," she laughed. "Sounds like a comic book title."

"Missy," said the clerk. "I like your sarcasm. You have spunk. But if I may give a word of advice--- Watch how you talk to the sheriff. He's a good guy, but doesn't have much of a sense of humor."

"Gotcha," Sheila remarked.

"Anytime ya want me." said the clerk with a grin.

Yessiree, thought Sheila, I definitely like this old codger.

"By the way," said Sheila as the clerk turned to leave. "What is your name?"

"It's Shecky." came the reply as he walked down the steps.

I definitely like that old bastard, thought Sheila as she put the towels on the bed.

Sheriff Richard Monte was short for a lawman, barely five-six and thin in frame.

Not exactly Clint Eastwood, she thought.

Sheila Barton tried everyway she could think of to refrain from making any short jokes, biting her lip seemed to be the only--- and most painful--- way to succeed in that endeavor.

"Now, Ms. Barton," said Monte.

"Sheila,"

"Ms. Barton," continued the sheriff, ignoring her offer of informality. "I know you're a reporter. Clyde over to the boarding house told me about you."

"Clyde?" asked Sheila, forgetting she wasn't alone. "His name's Clyde?"

"Pardon me?"

"Sorry," apologized Sheila.

"Anyway, I know you're investigating the animal attacks we've had in these here parts."

"Animal attacks, right." she couldn't hide the sarcasm in her tone of voice.

"Well, what do you think they are, Ms. Barton?"

"Serial killings," she offered.

"What kinda killings?"

"Serial killings… You know, more than one and following a particular pattern."

"I have no clue what a serial killing is. But the coroner over to Hoon County stated that the people were attacked by an animal. Torn apart as if by fangs and claws… a man, no matter how clever, could ever do that."

"What if he devised a weapon of some sort that mimicked animal fangs and claws? Is that possible?"

"I suppose," said Monte. "But how..?"

"I don't know that yet."

"Well, Ms. Barton, I don't have a problem with someone other than myself trying to get to truth here. But I must warn you, those woods are dangerous. You go out there after dark and you could get lost, fall down a chasm or get killed by a wild animal."

"I appreciate your concern, but I have to find out what killed those people. Call it an obsession. But I must know."

"Obsessions end up consuming the person afflicted with them. Sometimes, you just have to know when to walk away."

Sheila thought on that for a moment. What would she prove to herself if she did find out the truth behind those killings? Was this quest for answers really worth her life? She certainly didn't have many people backing her in this investigation. Nobody was impeding her either. But she just wasn't seeing much support in the actual pursuit. Maybe Adam could've helped.

…If he hadn't collapsed that building on top of his head.

"Well, Sheriff Monte," she said at last. "I may regret finding out the truth. But at least I'll know one way or another, what happened to those poor people."

Monte stood, not that it made much difference and extended his hand. Sheila took it and realized for the first time, that although Monte was small, he had a hell of a grip.

"Good luck, Ms. Barton. And may God protect ya."

Sheila smiled and started to leave the sheriff's office, but stopped at the doorway.

"One thing," the lady reporter said. "Is this Hoon County or not?"

"Merced is a part of Hoon County, yes. But the actual killings took place outside the city limits."

"Oh, good. I thought I was in the wrong place."

Sheila left the Sheriff's office and observed the last rays of the day's sun disappearing behind the mountains.

The sun was going down, she muttered, and the hunt was about to begin.

CHAPTER 9

Sheila placed her suitcase on the bed and pulled her .38 revolver from out of its hidden compartment. She'd only shot the thing once or twice, but it didn't matter; serial killer or wild animal, a bullet was a bullet.

She put a thick coat on and tucked her jeans into her heavy-weather boots. Now she looked like a hunter on the prowl. And yet, Sheila thought of one final modification that had to be made; her hair would be a detriment to her progress--- she hated the idea, but she knew that it had to go.

Grabbing a pair of scissors out of her bag, Sheila did the one thing all women dread…

She cut her hair!

Now, Sheila looked at herself in the mirror, almost threw up and gazed down at all the hair lying around her on the floor.

All right, she told herself, it will grow back. It's only hair. My hair, thought Sheila, my beautiful hair.

The lady hunter slapped her face with a hard open-handed smack. The blow bringing her to her senses, and after rechecking the revolver to make sure it had ammo, the intrepid lady reporter left the room.

Down in the lobby, Shecky dozed as he leaned on his elbow which in turn lain upon the counter.

Making no noise, Sheila crept past him, and turning the door knob ever so slowly, snuck out of the door and into the brisk night air. As soon as she stepped fully into the night, a cool breeze blowing in from the mountains made Sheila tighten the collar of her coat even more.

Well, here goes, she said to herself. And the fearless (yeah, right!) lady reporter began that long trek towards the woods wherein lie the truth to her investigations.

…And maybe certain death.

The path Sheila found could've been man-made; it certainly seemed too straight and narrow for it to be natural. In any case, she kept to the path and tried to deviate as little as possible.

She checked out the flora that spread before her in all directions, but in the darkness of night, she couldn't see much of anything except the pale moon hanging high above her. Uneasy and somewhat unnerved, Sheila reached down and slipping her hand into her coat pocket, she pulled out her flashlight and swept it in a tight circumference around her immediate area.

The woods appeared devoid of all life, save a few creepy-crawlies skittering over a rock or branch. Good thing she grew up in the country, the brave lady reporter told herself.

But a noise slightly to her left made her involuntarily jump in fright. Sheila killed the light and let her eyes readjust to the dark. Plus, she thought, no reason to give whatever the hell's out there a bead on her.

If you want me, nutso, you're going to have to work for it.

Sheila waited with bated breath, afraid to move even an inch; lest she give away her position. Seconds passed into minutes and still nothing came for her. But even now she dare not move.

It was time to bring out the gun, she thought. Slowly, very slowly, she slipped the revolver out of her pocket.

Sheila held the weapon in her right hand, reinforcing her shooting arm with the other hand. No Wyatt Earp one-handed shooting here, she said to herself.

Now, she felt ready for whatever was going to happen.

At least, she thought she was.

How could she describe what happened next?

It defied all convention and she doubted her sanity as well.

The figure came from the darkness like a speeding projectile forcefully ejected from a wide, gaping maw. She could see little of its form; nothing visible to her but two glowing eyes!

Adam? She asked herself.

No, couldn't be.

But those eyes! …Again a pair of glowing eyes.

These eyes appeared different though. She could see they were yellow, and animalistic. Like a wolf in the night, thought Sheila.

A wolf! That's it, she congratulated herself, you've solved the mystery. It's a wolf.

A wolf, my ass, Sheila corrected her mistake in deduction. The thing that stood before her was bipedal. Not on four legs, but erect like a human. This was a wolf-like being!

Whatever it was, Sheila had less than two seconds to either: A. Scream; B. Shoot; or C. Move.

The beast sprang! Quicker than she could pull the trigger!

It was upon her in a flash, knocking the revolver loose from her grip and sending the intrepid reporter tumbling to the ground. Sheila slammed onto the hard dirt, the impact knocking the wind out of her as she waited for the inevitable attack…

But it never came.

Sheila thought she could hear the sounds of a fierce struggle.

Someone was actually fighting with the beast?! She couldn't believe anyone could be so brave--- or suicidal. But who could possibly take the fight to a werewolf?

Only one name came to mind: Adam.

It had to be him, she told herself; no mere human could go up against a werewolf and actually make a difference. But Adam could--- he wasn't constrained by human weakness--- he didn't succumb to fear and pain.

Afterall, he dropped an entire building on his head and apparently came out unscathed.

It had to be Adam!

Against her better judgment (and concern for Adam), Sheila's curiosity overtook her fear and she made up her mind to help in any way possible. Following the battle to its source of origin, the lady reporter saw something she would never forget...

43

wo black shapes, one indiscernible from the other, struck at one another with such speed and ferocity that Sheila could not tell which one was the beast and which one her savior; to her disappointment, she also couldn't make out who was winning.

One thing she knew for certain--- neither had the monstrous build of Adam.

Their movements were so blindingly fast, they defied her ability to give even a semblance of an accurate description--- both combatants moved with lightning-quick reflexes, like two large jungle cats in dispute over territorial domination.

Finally, one of them broke away from the death match, having sighted, or sniffed, easier prey to rend with fang and claw.

Now Sheila knew which of the two had been the beast; the one barreling at her like a bat out of hell!

The lady reporter thought about running, but in her heart she knew the beast would get her no matter what kind of evasive action she took. Sheila Barton, aged 32, closed her eyes and prepared for her encroaching death--- praying to whatever deity was listening, it would, at the very least--- be over quick.

And yet again, the end did not come.

Wasting no time, the other black shape had pounced into the air and covered over five yards in one leap, coming down hard on the back of the beast's neck. This time; however, when the werewolf got back to its padded feet, the beast fled in defeat... maybe even having suffered an injury in the fierce battle.

Sheila watched it run off into the hills with a combination of relief and frustration. She had come so close to death, but at least now she knew the answer to the unexplained animal attacks.

But the lady reporter had another task in front of her now--- to thank her unknown, and largely unseen, protector.

A quick glance about her told Sheila this would not be an easy task to accomplish.

Her mysterious guardian had disappeared as well. But where could he have gone? There's really nowhere to hide, though Sheila, except--- Sheila craned her neck to look above her, noting all the thick tree branches that criss-crossed and/or ran parallel to each other; a highway in the sky, so to speak.

"Great," she said, exasperated. "I've just been saved by Tarzan."

"Not quite, Sheila," came a voice from out of the darkness. Sounding somewhat muffled to the lady reporter's ears.

"Does *everybody* know my name?" she asked sarcastically. "I'm not exactly wearing a nametag."

"I've known your name since you were a little girl." said the voice in the trees.

Sheila felt light-headed from staring up into the dark trees, so she lowered her head to clear the haze forming around the edges of her vision.

"Would you mind coming down out of the trees?" he requested. "If I look up any longer, I feel like I'm definitely going to pass out."

Just a few feet to her right, Sheila heard the softest of footfalls. Kinda light on his feet, she thought. Nevertheless, she decided she needed to thank him anyway.

"I'm grateful to you for saving my life."

"Think nothing of it," said the nameless shape.

"Now what was it you said about knowing me?" she prodded.

"I've been with you since the day we first met; when you were but a little girl, sitting by a creek."

Sheila almost fell over at this revelation. Had she truly and finally met the nameless man-thing from her childhood encounter?

"You're the mystery man?" she asked with noted skepticism.

"I am," he responded.

She still wasn't convinced. "Prove it."

"How?" inquired the mystery man.

"Tell me what I was wearing that day, all those years ago. I never forgot it. Let's see if you did."

If, she added under her breath, you are who you say you are.

The mystery man sighed and began to describe, in great detail, what little Sheila had been wearing that day, all those years ago:

"You had on a flowered dress, white socks and black buckled shoes, the kind with the hard soles. Your hair was in a ponytail and you had a flower resting snugly within a few strands of your dark locks, just slightly above your right ear. Don't ask me what type of flower it was because I've never been good with naming those things."

Tears were running down Sheila's cheeks--- she had been waiting twenty-some years for this moment. However, she could not tell if she now cried tears of joy or lamentation for a childhood long-past.

"How long have you been following me?" she asked, the reporter in her taking charge.

"Since the day we met." said the mystery man.

"That's a little creepy," Sheila pointed out.

"Only to ensure your safety," the mystery man stated.

"Do you watch me sleep too?" she asked bluntly.

"No, when you sleep, I sleep." he said. "When you're in danger, I intervene."

"But how is it I've never seen you in all this time? I *am* an investigative reporter you know."

"I'm older and trickier," remarked the mystery man, with a hint of wicked humor.

"Would you come out of the shadows?" asked Sheila. "I've been waiting years to see your face. I seem to have either forgotten, or repressed the memory of what you look like."

"You haven't forgotten, or repressed, anything, Sheila."

Sheila was glad to hear this bit of news, but it didn't make sense.

"How could that be?"

"You've *never* seen my face. Nobody has… for a very long time."

"Do you wear a mask or something?" she asked, trying to come up with a plausible reason.

"Yes," he said, matter-of-factly.

"Are you disfigured?"

"You could say that." he answered, rather vaguely.

"I'm sorry," said Sheila, and she meant it.

"Why?" asked the mystery man. "You had nothing to do with it."

"I know, but…"

"Ah, sympathy." he said, seemingly touched by the gesture. "Much appreciated. But unneeded, I assure you. I've had a long time to get used to what I am."

"So, what made you take an interest in my life? I mean, why me?"

The mystery man seemed to reflect on this point for a moment and after some deliberation, answered in his signature muffled voice.

"I saw you, at 9 years old or so, sitting by a creek and holding a small doll. You seemed to be talking to others on either side of you--- imaginary friends, I figured. Immediately, my heart was touched. I knew what it was to not have friends; to experience utter loneliness and neglect, day in and day out. At that moment, I felt we were kindred spirits.

"So I stood before you and when you did not scream or run away in panic, we became the other's only true companion."

Sheila wasn't sure what to make of the mystery man's account, but it seemed likely enough.

However, she did feel just a bit weirded-out by the whole "relationship".

"But I was a little girl. Don't you find that a bit creepy? I mean, a grown man and a ten-year-old child."

"We kept each other company, that's all." said the mystery man, obviously offended by her callous remark.

"I never knew your name," she said.

"You gave me a name," he said. "It was the name of one of your imaginary friends--- 'Ravenswood'."

The sound of that name made Sheila smile from ear to ear. She remembered it quite well.

"Raven's Wood," she said proudly. "He was... a Tree-Man. And he carried a flock of birds on his branch-like arms. He was my--- protector."

"You always did have a very vivid imagination, Sheila."

"Speaking of protecting," she said. "Thanks again for saving me from that beast."

"I told you. If you're in trouble, I intervene."

"Then where were you the other night?"

"Excuse me?" asked Ravenswood, sounding genuinely confused.

"When I was at that dive bar," she clarified. "And that extremely large man saved me from some drunken creep. Where were you then?"

"I was there," said Ravenswood flatly. "If the large man had not jumped in, I would've saved you; surreptitiously, of course."

"Of course," said Sheila, anger welling up at the gall of this masked man. "Listen, I appreciate you watching over me, but my name is not Lois Lane. So back off, will you?"

"Sheila, you misunderstand me. I haven't saved you every time you were in physical peril." said the masked man. "I didn't want you to depend on anybody but yourself when you got in trouble."

"Good." Sheila said proudly.

"I did, however, see you get taken away by that large man. And I watched that beautiful woman walk away with that bookish fellow as well."

"What?" said Sheila, astonished. "You saw where Professor Hague was taken?"

"Kind of, if that was the bookish fellow's name," replied Ravenswood.

"What does that mean?"

"I saw the woman lead him to a large silver limousine and drive off….Strange-looking vehicle, very ornate. Not one for being inconspicuous, this woman."

"Did you see which way the limo went?" asked Sheila anxiously.

"No, I had a choice ahead of me." said Ravenswood coldly. "Follow them or make sure you were safe."

"And naturally, you chose the latter." said Sheila in a harsh tone.

"I didn't know the man or the woman." The masked man stated. "What care did I have for his welfare when I was concerned about yours?"

"I was fine." Sheila snapped. "You saw the large man was no threat to me! You should've followed the limo!"

"Why? What matter is the man or woman to me?" asked Ravenswood, clearly clueless.

"That man was an expert in the occult." she explained. "If you had saved him; I wouldn't be here and I wouldn't have nearly been sliced apart by a frickin' werewolf!"

"I'm sorry," said Ravenswood. "I'll leave you alone now."

"Wait," said Sheila, softening a bit. "I'm sorry I yelled at you. Again, thanks for saving me tonight."

"Always," came Ravenswood's voice, once more above her, hidden in the trees.

Sheila laughed as the weight she'd been bearing on her soul and psyche for over twenty years was finally lifted. She at last knew she wasn't crazy, but it was strange that Ravenswood did not have glowing eyes.

Where had that delusion come from?

Sheila got back to the boarding house well after one in the morning. She was sore and exhausted from her ordeal. But she had a story to write and a conversation with Sheriff Monte in her immediate future.

The observant reporter noted that Shecky wasn't standing, or slumping, behind the counter anymore. She wondered if he slept in one of the rooms himself. There certainly were enough to spare.

Sheila walked up the stairs and went in her room. Flipping on the light switch, she nearly had a heart attack as she noticed a person sitting in the chair by her window.

"Oh, shit," she cursed.

"Evening, Ms. Barton," said Sheriff Monte. "Any luck in your hunt for the truth?"

"Sheriff, why the hell are you sitting in the dark? Are trying to perfect your Bela Lugosi impression?"

"Who?" asked Sheriff Monte, undoubtedly confused.

"Never mind," Sheila said, leaving the door open and walking over to sit on the edge of the bed.

"What do you want, Sheriff?" she asked, facing him.

"What did you find out, out there?" he inquired. "Was your theory correct?"

"If I told you what happened out there, you wouldn't believe me."

"Try me," Sheriff Monte prodded. He seemed truly interested in knowing the details.

"Okay," Sheila acquiesced. "There is something out in those woods…Something horrible, deadly…Some kind of beast that kills any one who enters its domain."

"Really?" asked the sheriff, stone-faced as ever; making it impossible for Sheila to tell if he was buying one word of her outrageous tale.

"Please continue." he said.

"I don't know what more to say." she sighed, exhausted from her ordeal. "The beast out there is dangerous. It should be hunted down and destroyed… before any more people are mauled to death."

"Ms. Barton, I am one man. I am the whole Sheriff's Department. How would you suggest I go about tracking down and killing a wild beast that thinks and reasons like a man?"

"Could you form a posse?"

"..Out of who, Clyde and you? There is no one else here in Merced."

"Then why do you and Clyde stay here?"

"We're family."

"No wives or children? No other relatives?"

"They're dead." said Sheriff Monte, sullenly.

Now Sheila understood everything.

"So, you two are just waiting, huh?"

"Yes."

Monte stood up and walked to the door, he lowered his head as he spoke.

"My boys were only 15 and 18. Clyde's son and daughter were both in their late twenties..."

The rest of the sheriff's sentence didn't need to be voiced.

"I'm so sorry," said Sheila, sincerely touched by his sadness.

"Have a good night, Ms. Barton." said Sheriff Monte.

Stopping in the open doorway, he turned to look at her with tear-filled eyes.

"I want you out of this hellhole by tomorrow. Me and Clyde are done for, but you are young and pretty. Don't let this be *your* final resting place too."

Sheriff Monte left the room, leaving the lady reporter to reflect on the utter desolation these men must've been feeling since the loss of their loved ones.

CHAPTER **11**

Rider Hague cringed in fear as he listened to the sounds coming from downstairs.

It sounded as if some large beast were howling in pain or hunger.

Hague gulped as he walked toward the door, he was afraid but he was curious too. And he *had to know*, especially if those noises were what he believed them to be.

What he'd deduced from all those reports about the unexplained animal attacks in Hoon County: The culprit was neither animal nor human, but something more horrible than anything imaginable--- a werewolf, or some kind of were-creature.

Maybe, he reasoned, a she-wolf even.

Perhaps it was Krystyn? Or maybe even that gorgeous blond Heidi.

No reason it couldn't be either or both of them. Lycanthropy knows no gender, it strikes whoever it will--- like a cancer that consumes those afflicted.

Yes! thought Hague, that's why I'm here. These women knew I could jeopardize their existence and they kidnapped me to keep me from spoiling their plans. But to what end?

Was he to become just another victim? And which one became the beast? Krystyn seemed the more likely candidate; she was forceful and very sensual. But Heidi could just as easily be the she-wolf, her country manner a complete façade to hide her true nature. Oh, Robert Louis Stevenson, if you only knew the implications that your story hold here.

It was an actual case of Dr. Jekyll and *Mrs.* Hyde.

Or Miss, seeing as how neither woman appeared to be married. Hague couldn't imagine either of them submitting to a man's will and taking his last name, at the cost of their own identities.

So, Hague had figured it out, but what could he do about it? Krystyn possessed the power of hypnotic suggestion, just like---

And then it struck him!

She wasn't the beast, she was the handler. Heidi became the beast; Krystyn merely pointed her "pet" in the direction she wanted her to go.

Maybe he could play one against the other and slip away in the ensuing confusion. It was a long shot, but it was worth it. Afterall, what other choice did he have?

Breakfast is served promptly at seven every morning and dinner at seven every evening.

Why Seven? Hague knew the answer to that question as well. That number was very significant in countless tales of folk lore, some of which involved the curse of lycanthropy: it was believed, in certain ancient cultures, that the seventh son of the seventh son born on the seventh day in the seventh month, upon reaching maturity would be doomed to become a werewolf. Of course it was all superstition, and lycanthropy was just another word for a person's sexual awakening; but some cultures believed in the curse very deeply. And Rider Hague was not one to belittle anyone's beliefs.

Especially since everything in the werewolf superstition fell nicely into place with his current predicament.

And, Hague noted, he saw no silver in this room whatsoever.

He knew it was neither mere chance nor simple coincidence?

Not at all... He didn't believe in them. To his largely scientific and reasonably rational mind, two and two made four and nothing else made sense. And if he ignored all the facts before him, well then, two and two made eight.

But he felt that the number seven was probably more linked to Krystyn than Heidi; in witchcraft, like many other religions, seven meant great magical power. And those who knew how to harness it--- would be immensely adept at wielding such awesome power.

A soft knock at the door made Hague jump!

"Come in," he said in a nervous manner.

Krystyn stood in the open door wearing a long white gown, her jet-black hair and bronzed skin making her appear to be something right out of a dream.

More like a nightmare, thought Hague.

"Hello, Rider," she said. "I thought you'd be asleep."

"I find it much more difficult to sleep as the days pass," he said disdainfully.

If his rudeness bothered Krystyn, she didn't let it show. She merely smiled and entered the room.

"I know you know what's going on here," she said, her amber eyes peering into Hague's.

Maybe she was probing the depths of his very soul.

"Does that mean I'm too dangerous to keep alive?"

"You forget who I am," she said arrogantly. "I can wipe your mind clean of anything I want. I can make you forget your childhood, your adolescence--- even your first time. If I so desire."

Hague felt his heart sink to his feet; it was a fate *worse* than death, he murmured.

"Then I am to become your mindless slave?"

"I have much better uses for you, darling." she said with a wicked smile.

"Like what?"

"How much do you know about that reporter you were going to speak with?"

"I know she's good and follows up on leads."

"Indeed she does," Krystyn said. "A trait that almost got her killed tonight."

"What do you mean?"

"Well, I'm sure you figured out, Professor--- that all those mysterious attacks were from a werewolf."

"I did."

"And I'm sure a bright guy like you also figured out who the werewolf is."

"I have."

"I knew you would." Krystyn purred. "So, then, Mr. Hague--- you know Heidi is the werewolf. And she went out hunting tonight."

"I kind of figured that out by the sounds coming from downstairs."

"What you haven't figured out is how Barton survived her encounter with my wonderful she-wolf."

Hague had to admit, the fact that Sheila Barton wasn't dead after coming into contact with such a notoriously ferocious beast such as a werewolf was not easily explained.

"How did she survive?"

"I was hoping you could tell me."

"How would I know?" he asked incredulously.

"You're a bright guy, think about it."

"Maybe she had help." he said.

The answer came to him suddenly. "...Of course, that big guy from the other night. The one who…"

Then Rider Hague thought about something his mind had noted but was too clouded to remember upon its actual happening.

"The one who touched you," said the occultist professor. "And both of your bodies making contact injured the other. What was it Sheila called him? Oh, yes… Adam!"

"That cretin does not have one-tenth the power I possess." the raven-haired witch spat out.

"I don't understand," said Hague.

"And nor could your feeble mind grasp what I am. I am so much more than just some mere witch."

"I think I know what you are." Hague said haughtily.

"One more word and I will plant a suggestion in your mind to cut out your own tongue."

Hague knew that she meant it. He dared not even think what he had deduced about her origins---lest she read his mind.

"Good boy, Rider," said Krystyn. "You are smart enough to heed my warning."

"But back to the reporter, Barton." Hague said, trying to change the subject as quickly as possible. "What about her? Did that big guy help her scare off Heidi?"

"Heidi told me a most interesting tale," began Krystyn. "The thing helping Barton was masked. And more of a medium build…"

She looked at him with an accusatory glare. "About like you"

Hague laughed, was she really accusing him of being some kind of hero?

"Now how could I help her if I'm locked in here? I can't escape. And I'd fall to my death if I tried going out the window."

"Maybe you're tougher than you pretend to be."

"But surely, you could just read my mind. Then you would know it wasn't me."

"I did. And I know you're telling the truth. But it is getting annoying how many times some mysterious superhuman has come to that reporter's aid, every time I've tried to have her killed."

"Every time…?" asked Hague.

"At least twice now…" Krystyn clarified. "I've tried to silence that damn reporter and someone has stepped in to save her snoopy ass."

Aside from Heidi, who else attacked Sheila? And why do you want her dead?"

"I want her dead because she annoys me. Her probing into my business has forced my hand.

And as for your other question--- figure it out for yourself."

Finally, he understood.

"The drunk the other night?" said Hague triumphantly. "But he seemed to have all his faculties."

"I merely planted a suggestion in his mind. I didn't give him an actual command. He was already a big simple-minded ape; I just slightly nudged him in Barton's direction."

"Then how do you plan on eliminating her now? Her two guardians will be watching over her all the time now."

"One will, I know. But the other..."

Krystyn paced back and forth as she appeared to be cooking up another plan in her devious little mind. Then she appeared to be struck by an idea and stopped.

"Why didn't I think of this earlier?" she said, smiling.

"What?"

"I know how to get rid of that nosy reporter," said Krystyn, not bothering to look at him.

Then the raven-haired beauty swung around, her long gown swooshing like a great cape as she left the room, and Rider Hague, without uttering another word.

Nosy reporter, the professor said silently, you've been watching too many B-movies, lady.

Hague woke up to Heidi standing over him, her long blond hair shimmering in the early morning sun. He could not believe that this angelic being was a demon clothed in human flesh.

"Morning," said Hague in a raspy waking voice.

"Mornin'," said Heidi, in her country twang.

"Breakfast time...?"

"No, not yet." she said, with a hint of depression. "You must come with me."

Hague didn't like the feel of her mood, he smelled something fishy in this whole set-up.

And he knew that a set-up, it was.

But what choice did he have? Fight off this wolf in sheep's clothing? And, if he succeeded--- then what?

Somehow defeat the High Priestess of Set and make an escape?

Every scenario led to his death or permanent maiming. He had no choice but to follow the she-wolf, or "Ms. Hydee", to wherever Krystyn commanded.

"I will do as you ask,"

"Ms. Krystyn said you would."

Yeah, Ms. Krystyn knows all, doesn't she? mumbled Hague under his breath.

How I'd like to put a stake through her black heart. What was he saying? She was probably reading his mind at that very moment. He'd practically just signed his own death warrant.

Oh, well, thought Hague, he'd find out once he was face to face with that--- that---

Rider Hague knew what she really was, but he dared not finish the sentence.

Rider Hague was allowed to see, for the first time, the rest of the house he'd been locked up for days. The hallway alone was grand; unbelievably long and seemingly endless; branching off into several different directions and leading to yet another series of rooms.

The balustrade stretched out to his left and dipped down as it followed the aesthetic design of the staircase. Hague realized at last that he was inside a manor, a very large manor.

Nothing but the best for evildoers, he said to himself; live high off the hog in comfort and style while good people are torn from limb--- leaving barely a corpse to put in a cemetery plot.

Hague became angered as he thought more and more how these demonic women were living the good life, while all the people they had collectively killed were average, hard-working country folk. If he had more guts---

Heidi led him down the rather ornate staircase, which ended in a pair of grotesque newel posts on either side of him. Hague couldn't quite make out the design, but it seemed vaguely Egyptian in architecture.

Yes, his mind screamed, it was Egyptian!

But again, Hague pushed that thought from his mind. He wanted to stay focused and keep an eye open for any possible means of escape.

However, all those hopes were dashed when he noticed that beside each door stood a large, bare-chested man.

In fact, they barely wore any clothing at all--- a simple loincloth gave them a small measure of propriety. Krystyn liked degrading men--- that much was plain to see.

In a culture where the man is the supposed dominant member of the two genders, Hague had to admit a certain grudging respect for way Krystyn turned it all around in her little corner of the world.

"Through here," said Heidi.

"Right…"

As Heidi led Hague to a large study she seemed to emit a low growl from deep in her throat.

"Oh, no," she drawled. "It's happening before moonrise now."

"What is?" asked Hague.

"Nothing you need to worry about," she said, in a slightly different voice; more bestial than human.

Her eyes began to take on that animalistic glow again and Hague could see that her usually hairless body now adopted a more-shaggy look.

"Are you alright?" he asked, his voicing rising in pitch.

"I'm fine, little man," she said, her country twang now gone.

Heidi had indeed become a completely different person.

"How did you get like this? What happened to you?"

Heidi, or whoever she now was, glared at Hague with cold yellow eyes and sharp teeth, her once lovely hands now knotted, with each finger terminating into vicious-looking claws.

"Heidi," he said, concern in his voice.

"Don't ever call me that!" she commanded. "Heidi is a weak-willed little twink …A real corn-pone. I am a woman." the she-beast boasted.

"I'm **more** than a woman. I'm a goddess among sheep." said the creature, as it rubbed its body in an auto-erotic fashion.

"Then what do I call you?" asked Hague, slightly aroused by the spectacle.

"What need have I for a human name?"

"So you are the wolf-goddess?" offered Hague.

"How about… 'Goddess-Wolf'?" asked the female werewolf.

"W-W-Whatever you say," Hague stammered.

"That's right, little man, whatever I say."

"I think it's whatever **I** say?"

Both of them knew the voice of Krystyn as soon as they heard it.

"Your power only affects men, witch." said the wolf-goddess.

"My powers of suggestion, maybe… But I have much more power than that at my command."

Goddess-Wolf made a move toward Krystyn, a move of aggression. Yet the raven-haired sorceress did not look beleaguered in the least. "Now, now," she said, her voice sickeningly sweet. "You and I make such a good team. Why break up the relationship at this juncture?" "Because," snarled the she-beast. "I'm through taking orders from you!"

"But my dear 'Goddess-Wolf', I want to give you no orders. I merely want you to help me get rid of that nosy reporter. You know… the one you failed to kill last night."

Krystyn stuck the verbal dagger in deep enough that the wolf-goddess could not help but feel the sting of the witch's words.

Goddess-Wolf threw back her hairy-head and howled to the ceiling, a mixture of anger or disappointment. Hague noted that Krystyn definitely knew how to use words as a weapon.

And as the occult professor watched the comely sorceress weave a web of surreptitious phrases and suggestions around her bestial counterpart, he could see the anger in the wolf-goddess' eyes turn to sheer and utter jubilation.

Now, both "women" turned their respective gazes on him.

Shit, he thought, I don't like the looks of this.

Krystyn and Goddess-Wolf made their way to where he stood and Rider Hague wished he had the power to make himself invisible so that he could leave their demonic presence forever.

CHAPTER 12

Sheila sat at the train depot waiting for her eleven o'clock departure time.

She reflected on everything that had happened to her in the last few days and the sheer strangeness of it all. The lady reporter couldn't grasp the odds of someone meeting two beings of supernatural origin and barely escaping death at the hands (or claws) of an actual werewolf.

Her mind raced as she tried to wrap her brain around it all.

And Ravenswood was probably hiding somewhere right now, watching her; making sure nobody, or no thing, brought her any harm.

And what of Adam, she thought. Was he truly dead? Sure, a building fell on him, but seeing as how he was somewhat less, and yet more, than human--- could he still be alive somewhere in the city? Maybe hiding in another condemned building, staying out of sight of frightened human eyes. Eyes that would surely judge based solely on his outer appearance, just as they had judged Ravenswood on his.

How could she ever tell anybody about her life? Would Eggy buy her story? It was all true, but even she didn't believe half of it. And she was there!

The lady reporter reflected on Adam and Ravenswood: a reptilian-like proto-human and a masked guardian with shades of the Phantom of the Opera?

Sheila felt her face turning red, and knew she needed a cigarette.

In the excitement over the last few days, she'd almost forgotten she smoked.

What a crime!

An announcement over the P.A. startled the lady reporter as she shuffled through her purse looking for her cigarettes and lighter.

"What the hell are you using that for?" she screamed at the clerk.

"Just trying to see if you were still awake, Missy."

She knew that voice, the sarcastic tone and with its slight twang. It was Shecky!

Sheila jumped off the bench and ran to the office. Clyde Monte met her before she even had a chance to open the door.

"I was afraid I wouldn't get a chance to say goodbye." he said, a bit choked up.

"Not on your life, you old codger…"

"Richard told me he gave you an order to leave town."

"Richard?" she asked. "Oh--- the sheriff."

"Yeah, ol' Rich and me are cousins. Both of our fathers was brothers."

"Listen," said Sheila, not knowing how to say what she wanted. "He told me about your kids. I'm really sorry."

"Yeah," said Clyde. "Me too… His kids weren't even out of their teens yet."

"Why don't you two leave this town and come with me?"

"To the city?" asked Clyde, incredulous. "Missy, I was born in Merced. And this is where I will die."

"But why?" she couldn't understand either man's stubbornness to leave certain death behind.

"What have I got anymore? Except Rich… and he'd never leave Merced either. …Stubborn as mule, that man."

"If you ask me, you're both bull-headed."

Clyde hugged Sheila as if saying goodbye verbally was not going to be possible.

Before she could respond, the old man let go and walked away.

Sheila looked after him until he disappeared into the Sheriff's office. The lady reporter wiped a tear from her cheek as she thought about the horrible fate that awaited the men.

Then suddenly she was struck by an idea--- their salvation was within her grasp. She had her own personal superhero at beck and call. Ravenswood!

Ravenswood could watch over Clyde and Rich; keep them safe when the beast returned to finish them off. He was the only one capable of defeating the beast and protecting them from its feral wrath.

Sheila looked up on the roof of the depot, hoping to see her hidden guardian crouching there like some human spider or living gargoyle. But alas, the roof was devoid of anything but shingles and regular-sized spider webs.

Damn, she thought, never around when you really need him. Desperate and lacking time, Sheila did the only thing she could think of.

She yelled for him.

"Ravenswood…!"

No response.

Damn! Damn him, she mumbled to herself. Where the hell could he be?

"Ravenswood, damn it, I need you!"

"I gathered," said the masked guardian.

Sheila nearly jumped out of her skin at the sound of his muffled voice coming from *inside* the depot. She peered into the dimly-lit lobby, barely making out his dark form.

"How long have you been standing there?" she demanded.

"Long enough," he said cryptically.

"Long enough for what…?"

"To see you are worried about those two men …The sheriff and the innkeeper."

"That's right," she said adamantly. "And I want to ask you a favor."

"You have but to ask, Sheila." said Ravenswood, and she could tell he meant it.

"Those two guys are nice guys. They treated me very kindly while I stayed here. I'd hate to think that they are to be killed once the sun goes down tonight."

"And you want me to watch over them?"

"Yes," she said with great enthusiasm.

"I cannot." was Ravenswood's terse reply.

"Why the hell not...?"

"Because... I don't care about them. Your safety alone is paramount to me."

"But don't you understand? Those two innocent men are going to be devoured when that beast gets into town tonight."

"I understand perfectly, Sheila," said Ravenswood in a cold tone. "But their well-being is of no concern to me."

"Well, it's of a major concern to me!" she exclaimed. "And if you won't help them, then don't bother talking to, or stalking, me anymore!"

Sheila turned to leave, but a strong hand gripped her arm.

"If it means that much to you," said Ravenswood. "I will do as you ask."

"Thank you, Ravenswood. It **does** mean a lot to me."

Sheila noticed for the first time that Ravenswood had on pair of dark goggles over his eyes, the overall effect making him resemble some kind of giant bug, or maybe Claude Rains in his most famous role. She also thought she could almost make out the faintest glow behind those opaque eye-coverings.

"Why are you wearing those dark glasses?" she asked.

"That is of no concern to you, little girl." he answered in a brisk manner.

"I'm sorry, I didn't mean to pry."

"Of course, you did. That is who you are. ...Who you have always been. And that is why you weren't afraid of me when we met all those years ago."

Ravenswood let go of Sheila's arm and melted back into the heavily shadowed lobby.

"And that is why I will watch over the Montes as you have asked."

Sheila smiled as she watched her mysterious guardian disappear from view.

Maybe not so much the Phantom of the Opera, she told herself.

But still kinda creepy, she added.

Krystyn stood next Rider Hague, his clouded mind barely comprehending what the raven-haired witch was saying to him. But her powers made it possible for him to at least follow his mistress' commands.

"There's that nosy bitch," said Krystyn, anger barely contained in her sensual voice.

"I don't care if you kill her, but either way I want her body brought back to me at Pike Manor."

The two of them were hidden in the shadows of the abandoned station house, watching Sheila Barton like a couple of voyeurs as they pretty reporter stepped onto the awaiting train.

"She really is quite lovely, isn't she?" asked Krystyn, more of a rhetorical question than anything else.

"I've changed my mind. Bring her back to me alive. I think I could have a lot of fun with her."

Hague only slightly understood the double meaning of Krystyn's statement. But even in his fugue state he was inherently aroused by the thought of what the two of them could do to each other.

"Now, get on that train." said his raven-haired controller.

Without uttering a word, Rider Hague did as ordered and hopped on the slowly departing locomotive.

He was a slave to the mad woman's every whim and there was nothing he could do about it except obey.

As he boarded, the mind-controlled occultist thought he spotted a dark shape crouching on the station house roof. But he dismissed the crazy illusion and made his way into the passenger car.

While on the train moving away from Merced, Sheila found herself unable to do anything but gaze out of the window, watching the rolling hills flash by in the blink of an eye.

"May I sit here?"

Sheila slowly looked up to see who had addressed her and nearly fell out of her seat.

Professor Rider Hague!

"Yes," she said, trying to find her voice. "Please do."

"Thank you," he said.

The lady reporter gazed at him; he looked no worse for wear. No bruises or cuts, no teeth missing, all his fingers, both of his eyes and ears. No physical damage that could be discerned by visual study.

But, she reasoned, what of mental trauma?

Afterall, he had been kidnapped and held hostage somewhere for at least 48 hours.

And how had he escaped?

Sheila didn't like the feeling she was getting from the newest wrinkle of this increasingly-confounding case. She didn't like it at all.

And--- she knew a trap when she saw one.

"So, Mr. Hague, how did you manage to escape your captor?"

"My captor?" he asked, somewhat mechanically.

Sheila observed his manner of being with her investigative eye; the professor looked stiff--- almost robotic. As if he were put under a trance or something.

A trance!

Yes, now it all made sense. Whoever kidnapped him--- brainwashed him and for whatever reason, had decided to use him as bait for a trap. A trap meant to ensnare her! Sheila mentally congratulated herself; have to get up pretty early in the morning to put one over on Sheila Barton, Ace Investigative Reporter.

"As I was saying Mr. Hague," she continued. "How did you get away from the lady you were with? Not that any sane man would consciously want to get away from that living doll. But how did you do it?"

"I don't know what you mean, Ms. Barton."

Sure you don't, she thought, and I don't have small breasts.

"If you say so, Mr. Hague…"

Time for a different tact, she told herself.

"Heading back to the city?"

"No."

"Where are you going then?"

"Home," came the monotone reply.

"I thought you lived in the city."

"No." Again Sheila noted that Hague spoke in a disconnected manner.

"Where's home?" she asked, prodding for more information.

"Home is," he said. "Home is where the heart is."

"Very funny, Mr. Hague," said Sheila, voice oozing sarcasm.

Fine, have your way. But she knew for certain she was not going anywhere this man suggested. Or was she?

Sheila thought about the implications: here was a professor with knowledge of the occult and he was kidnapped by a beautiful woman, held hostage while the woman or her cronies brainwashed him and then sent to lead her into a trap.

But why her? Had she uncovered something more than even she realized?

Had this something to do Hoon County and the beast?

Was this mysterious beauty somehow involved in it all? Perhaps she was the beast or maybe someone close to her. …A husband, perhaps?…Or a brother? Maybe even a son.

What about a daughter? It wasn't entirely implausible for a female to be a werewolf. She'd read old folklores about several women and men becoming a pack of werewolves and hunting down people like the animals for which they were named. Could the beast in fact be a *beastess*?

Then how did Professor Hague fit in all this?

Maybe she would go along with whatever this woman had planned afterall. But first, she had to get a message to Eggy. Tell him the whole story before it died with her. She owed that much to the unsuspecting public. At least, if she ended up being killed, people would know the *truth* and not rest until they hunted down, and **destroyed**, the mysterious woman--- along with her pet werewolf.

"Excuse me, Mr. Hague," said Sheila as she rose from her seat.

"Where are you going?" he inquired in his robotic tone.

"If I want somebody asking my business, I'll get married."

Hague gave no reaction to her insult and simply stared forward in his trance-like state. Sheila noted that he seemed to have no orders to forcefully impede her, so it made it that much easier for her to use the train's mobile phone.

After making the necessary deposit of coins, Sheila was connected with the main offices of the People's Gazette.

They then transferred her call to the newsroom and from there to Eggy's extension.

"News editor's office… Eggy Quayles speaking."

"Hiya, Eggy," said Sheila. "How's every little ting?"

"Barton?" he said, and she could almost see his eyes popping out of his head.

"Yeah, boss, it's me."

"Where are you?"

"…On a train heading for the city." said Sheila; then added. "… Maybe."

"What the hell does that mean?"

"It means, I have something amazing to tell you. You just won't believe it when I tell you."

"What?" now Quayles sounded intrigued.

"I solved the mystery of those animal attacks."

"You didn't." he said, full of skepticism.

"I did, Eggy."

"So, was your theory correct? Was it a serial killer?"

"Yes and no."

"What do you mean 'yes and no'?"

"I mean…" how could she tell him without sounding like a complete loon?

"Well…?" he said eagerly. "Tell me, will ya? The suspense is killing me."

"The animal attacks were not done by an animal, per se."

"Then it was a *maniac* committing ritual killings."

"No, it wasn't that either. Those people were killed by an animal-like attacker."

"Animal-like… what does *that* mean?"

"It means, Eggy, that they were killed by a human-like animal."

"Now, I'm really confused. First, you tell me it wasn't a man, now you say it wasn't an animal, but it was like a man?"

"Something like that, yes." Sheila felt sorry for poor Eggy, she was probably increasing his blood pressure with every sentence.

"Sheila, just tell me what the hell you found out." he said finally.

"Eggy, it was a werewolf."

She was greeted by absolute silence on the other end.

"Eggy?" she asked, thinking they'd got disconnected. "…You still there?"

"Yes, Barton, I'm still here. But are you?"

"What's that supposed to mean?"

"Are you still on this planet?" he bellowed. "Or have you flown off on a rocket ship straight to cuckoo land?!"

Sheila pulled her ear away from the phone as quickly as she could, but not quick enough to avoid the stinging from Eggy's outburst.

"I'm telling you, Eggy. It was a werewolf, I saw it! It attacked me!"

"What?" he said, voice full of concern. "Are you alright?"

"Yes, I'm fine."

"How did you escape an attack from a "supposed" werewolf?"

"Well, that part of the story is much harder to explain. You see, I had some help."

"Oh, got it. Local law enforcement saved you, right?"

"Not exactly…"

"Here we go again."

Sheila had to laugh at Eggy's exasperation.

"Eggy, all you need to know is that I found the answers to several of my questions out in those woods."

"Like the meaning of life, I suppose."

"Don't be ridiculous."

"Oh, that's rich," said Eggy. "…*You*, telling me not to be ridiculous. Sometimes I think your middle name is 'Ridiculous'."

"That's absurd," said Sheila. "You know my middle name is 'Hard-Ass'."

Now it was Eggy's turn to laugh.

"…Right."

"I'll see you soon, Eggy."

"Take care, kiddo."

Sheila hung up with a minute to spare. Maybe the story would die with her.

Oh, well, thought Sheila, now to find out what Professor Rider Hague can tell me about a certain werewolf and its keeper.

Back inside the train car, Rider Hague tried desperately to fight off the trance he'd been placed in.

He felt as if he were in a dream, he could see himself doing everything; but could do nothing to control his own actions.

Whatever commands Krystyn had put in his psyche he had no choice but to obey. And the one thing that kept running through his mind was:

Bring Sheila Barton to me.

That was his assignment and God help him, he planned on carrying it out--- whether Barton wanted to go along or not. He had ways to get her to cooperate.

Had he really just thought that?

He wasn't violent and he certainly wasn't an assassin. But the command in his mind could not be ignored and he was told to use whatever means necessary to get her to Pike Manor--- and to his Mistress.

Hague moved his head at the sound of the passenger car door sliding open. He watched Sheila Barton step back into the cramped quarters and sit directly in front of him on the opposite seat.

She gazed into his eyes, trying to discern his mental state.

I'm fine, Ms. Barton, his mind told him. But you on the other hand, are mere hours from death.

If Sheila could read his thoughts, she didn't give any indication of knowing the dread peril her life was now in.

Rider Hague smiled at the lady reporter, who smiled back.

That's right, keep smiling, cause I've got a surprise for you.

CHAPTER 13

Sheila noticed that the train was making an unscheduled stop and looked out the window.

Before she could move, Rider Hague was behind her, bringing his arm across the back of her neck with more strength she imagined he could possess.

Rider Hague looked on Sheila Barton awoke in the same type of room he'd had been kept in for the last few days.

The occultist professor knew quite well the layout was basically the same: no furniture, save a bed; a bathroom to the right and a locked door leading out to a second story balcony.

Hague stared down at Barton with a mixture of disgust and lust. He scanned his eyes over her thin, but well-shaped body… he noted her facial features and decided she was very pretty.

As he continued to ogle her prone form, Hague found himself reaching for her.

He touched his hand to her cheek, feeling how smooth the skin was on her youngish face. She was not a child, but she was definitely no hag either. She was a woman, through and through. And because she was a true woman, he felt a great longing to be with her; to feel her, to love her ---as only a man could.

Inside Hague's clouded mind, he knew he'd always found her desirable, but never had the nerve to tell her. Now, under the spell of some witch--- now he felt he could finally let Sheila know his feelings for her.

As he reached down to kiss her, Sheila Barton punched him in the face!

"That's what you get for slugging me when I wasn't looking!"

Sheila jumped off the bed and noticed she was wearing a very thin gown, with no bra and no panties. Talk about catching me with my pants down, she fumed.

"All right, buster," she said, grabbing Hague by his lapels. "Where am I?"

"In the houd of my Mitress," said Hague, hands going to his bloodied nose.

"Who's your mistress? What's her name?"

"I can'd dell you that." he said, still holding his nose.

"You want another pop in the face?"

"No," Hague said through his hands.

"Then spill. Why am I here?"

"I think I can answer that question better than him," said a voice as the door opened.

A sultry female voice, Sheila thought.

Sheila was not one to entertain thoughts of being with a woman, but the drop-dead gorgeous beauty who stood before her made the lady reporter think about giving it a shot.

"And just who are you, sister?" demanded Sheila, putting on a tough exterior.

"I am called Krystyn," said the raven-haired beauty.

"You're pretty hot, toots." Sheila commented with a wink.

"And you, my lovely, are no slouch either."

Sheila didn't know where this was heading, but she was having fun getting there.

"But I have not brought you here to bed you."

"Now, that's a damn shame."

Krystyn laughed at Sheila's brashness. She appeared interested, but distant.

"You have caused me much trouble, my lovely." said Krystyn, entering fully into the room.

The dark-haired beauty was wearing a bikini-like outfit, but much more elaborate. It showed off some nice cleavage and her killer legs. Sheila was almost jealous, but she didn't look bad in a bikini herself--- if the reaction she got from guys at the gym was any indication.

"So, how have I caused you much trouble, toots?"

Krystyn smiled. "Witty, aren't you?"

"I try."

"Indeed," came her dry response. "I would ask that you follow me downstairs to my parlor."

"Said the spider to the fly," mumbled Sheila.

"Something like that." Krystyn said.

In the parlor, Sheila noted Krystyn had a wealth of books in many shelves. She couldn't quite make out the names, but she figured one or two dealt with lycanthropy.

"Don't like to read much, do you?" said Sheila, voice dripping with her famous sarcasm.

"The time for levity is at an end, my lovely."

Krystyn pulled back a large curtain revealing a hidden door.

"Are you familiar with the 'Lady or the Tiger'?" asked Krystyn. "Wonderful story… Somewhat anticlimactic for me, but the theory is intriguing. Don't you think?"

"Let me guess, I'm to play 'Lady or the Beast', right."

"Something like that," remarked Krystyn. "But in my version there is no lady."

As Krystyn finished speaking those words, she hit a button on the wall that opened the large door in front of Sheila, or at least the lady reporter figured that was how the door opened by itself.

A bestial howl escaped the darkened recess, making Sheila regret not being more observant on the train.

The beast came out of the room at a slow pace, almost haughty in manner. This was no werewolf, thought Sheila. It was a demoness or something. It appeared almost human, but covered with long golden fur. It was somewhat attractive in a "wild-woman of Borneo" kind of way. Could this be the same ferocious beast from the previous night?

"So nice you could join us," said the wolf-woman, her voice raspy but not animalistic.

"Thanks," said Sheila, unsure of what to say.

"You caused me a lot of pain last night." said the wolfish female. "Your masked friend nearly broke my back. I didn't appreciate that."

"Sorry," said Sheila.

"Yes, well, the past is in the past, right?"

The wolf-woman now stood face to face with the lady reporter and Sheila felt as if she were going to piss herself right there.

"I was wondering," began the beast. "Would you happen to know where I might find your masked friend?"

"I...I...I don't r...really know at this t...time."

"Are you afraid of me, my dear?" asked the beast.

"Yes."

"Hmmm." said the wolf-woman, as if in thought. "And if I were to take my claws and rip you apart... Do you think I would derive great pleasure from such an act?"

"I don't know," Sheila said, scared beyond belief.

"You are a nosy reporter, is this not true?"

"Yes."

"And yet, here you are trembling before me. Am I so frightening to such a brave reporter?"

"I sup...suppose."

"Hmmm." said the wolf-woman again. "You suppose? Does that mean that you do have a bit of backbone after all?"

The wolf-woman placed her clawed hands on Sheila's breasts, cupping each in her talons.

"I've always wondered what it'd be like to take a woman." said the beast, licking Sheila's neck.

"I was always so pent up," the beast explained. "So afraid to try new things..."

Sheila wanted to faint, but her body had been conditioned to handle the stress of her job and besides, she was *not* some wilting flower.

The wolf-woman moved her bestial face down Sheila's chest, hovering just above her right nipple.

"Your body is firm, like a warrior's. You will not go without a fight, will you?"

How could she answer that? There would be no right answer. If she said no, the beast would attack.

If she said yes, then the beast would probably kill her outright.

"I don't need an answer, your silence tells me all I need to know."

The wolf-woman turned to Krystyn and smiled. "I think I will take her."

"That was not our deal," said Krystyn, fuming.

"To hell with your deal…! This woman is to be mine!"

Now the wolf-woman stared back at Sheila, her lips salivating as she looked over her "prey".

"But what of my plans?" asked Krystyn.

"And what are your plans, witch?" asked the beast. "I am driven by my appetites; both of them. What drives you?"

Krystyn grew silent.

"I have been charged with a task. And it must be completed for my continued longevity."

"What does that mean?"

"It means, you are the last of the unholy triumvirate."

Now, Sheila piped up. "What unholy triumvirate?"

But the wolf-woman growled at her and immediately silenced her curiosity.

"What unholy triumvirate are you talking about?" asked the wolf-woman. "…You, me and that slave of yours?"

"No, you beastly bitch!" screamed Krystyn. "If you must know: the vampire, the werewolf and the hybrid."

"What?"

"I was charged with bringing to life three of the most vile and inhuman creatures man has ever seen. I was given a vial with blood from a demon with which I could accomplish this task. The first one was the hybrid, a mixture between the old race and the new. He would be stronger than any man and have knowledge of eons past within his very being. He would be a clone of the demon, with the soul of a man."

Sheila understood the witch's description immediately--- a cross between demon and man; a being that was large, strong and grotesque to behold. The first one... Adam: The First.

"Who was the second?" asked Sheila.

Again the beast growled at her. This time she wasn't intimidated. "Save it, sister, okay! It's getting really old."

The wolf-woman looked at Sheila with surprise and amusement; then simply looked back at Krystyn.

"You heard the lady," said the beast. "Now answer her question."

"The second one was more difficult because it had to be a vampire," said Krystyn, her voice hollow. "And I had to find a well-preserved corpse to inject the demon's blood into. I needed to find a person who had died with a grudge, so their lust for blood would be immense. Word cameo me of a vain and violent young man who had been killed for his unholy crimes and his body was not allowed to be buried in the local cemetery."

The bronze-skinned witch began to pace as she continued her tale. "So the people carried his cursed body into the mountains and placed it in a cave ... The high altitudes and low temperature preserving the young man's corpse well beyond twenty years. Of course, decomposition eventually set in and his skin had deteriorated somewhat by the time I injected him with blood."

"Then what happened?" asked Sheila.

Krystyn didn't answer.

"What happened?" demanded the beast.

"He arose from his resting place in the cave and when I told him of his rebirth and showed him his decomposed face, he fled. Crying about his looks and the monster he became."

Sheila mind worked overtime, a supernatural being with a rotting face? Would that be the kind of person who would cover up their appearance for all eternity? Wear a mask over their deformity?

Vampires were said to be quick and strong, one could surely leap several feet in one bound; just as Ravenswood did the night prior. Sheila's mind screamed--- it was all beginning to make sense now.

"And the werewolf," said Sheila, trying to put the final piece to the puzzle in place. "How did you effect her transformation?"

"I can answer that," said the beast.

"I was born with a rare blood type; it is believed to have been directly derived from the bloodline of King Lycaon himself …known as the first werewolf. Krystyn here found me and offered to take me in. I had no family around here, being from Kentucky and all. So I agreed. Little did I know, she was going to stick me with some kind of needle--- that made my blood boil as soon as the moon would rise"

"The demon's blood, I bet." said Sheila, deducing what was in the syringe.

"Now, it all adds up. You and Adam burned at each other's touch. He is not to touch you, his creator, so to speak, and his touch is painful to you as well… just not as badly. So, if you were to touch the wolf-demoness here, the same thing would happen, right?"

"I answer none of your questions," said Krystyn.

"What I don't understand is your stake in all this."

"I do," said Rider Hague for the first time since they walked in the room.

CHAPTER **14**

"**M**r. Hague," said Krystyn in a warning tone. "Remember what I told you."

"I remember, but I think your powers are waning. Hence the seven victims you sacrificed."

"She sacrificed?" asked Sheila, completely thrown by the revelation. "I thought the wolf-woman here did that."

Now the wolf-goddess glared at Sheila for a change.

"No, our weakened sorceress here…" said Hague, pointing to Krystyn. "Sent the werewolf out to *gather* up victims, not kill. After she sacrificed them, she then ordered the werewolf to mangle their bodies so everyone would think it was a wild animal."

"Then who is she really?"

"A high priestess of ancient Egypt is my guess" said Hague. "Probably over thousands of years old… Possibly older than that… I'm no expert in Egyptology."

"That's right, you are not." said Krystyn in a haughty manner.

"But you are," stated Sheila.

"Do you think I would tell you my origins?"

"I've figured out enough to know you're dying." said Hague. "You were given a limited amount of time to complete your task and now, having failed your task, you are slowly aging. By the time you reach your true age, you'll be nothing but a pile of dust… like a well-preserved mummy when it is exposed to the oxygen in the air."

"That's not true," argued Krystyn. "I am eternal. I was around when the first 'human' made its unwanted debut and I will be here long after all of you are destroyed."

Hague noted the way Krystyn had pronounced the word "human" with such disdain.

"How so…?" asked Sheila. "You have no army or weapons."

"Are you so sure, 'Miss Mouth'?"

"I don't see any. Where are you hiding them--- under those huge boobs of yours?"

"I have the power of dark magic in my hands, derived directly from my 'Lord'. I need only speak the words and you will all fall before me."

"Enough of this!" yelled the wolf-woman. "I will take my prize and leave here now!"

With that, the beast grabbed Sheila's hand and began dragging her out of the room.

"Come back here, you clod!" Krystyn demanded; her amber eyes aflame. "I order you to kill her! She has to die!"

Sheila screamed as the beast drug her out of the room, asking Rider Hague to help her.

But Hague was no hero, and he had his own problems.

"So, Mr. Hague," said Krystyn, her amber eyes glowing. "You think you're so smart don't you?"

"I'm apparently not smart enough to figure a way out of this mess."

"That's right, you're not."

Krystyn, yanking a book from a nearby shelf, opened the tome and pulled a knife that had been hidden within a hollowed out page. She brandished the weapon at Rider Hague, and he knew she had every intention of slicing him up.

"Remember what I told you about making you cut out your own tongue?" she said with a leer.

"Yes," he gulped.

"I think I'd much rather do it myself. After all the trouble you have caused me tonight, I *know* I'd much rather do it myself."

The raven-haired priestess lunged at him, slicing his shirt but missing his skin.

"Come here, my slave." she hissed. "I'll make it quick if you don't make me chase you."

"Sorry, lady, you have to catch me before you kill me."

Hague ran out of the parlor and up the stairs, he could hear Sheila's screams coming from one of the rooms. What was that beast doing to her?

He shivered at the thought and nearly got a knife in the back thanks to his momentary lapse in attention. Krystyn looked like a woman possessed, her hair a wild mess atop her perfectly-shaped head, her bronze body gleaming with sweat. Hague almost found her attractive, even now as she was attempting to tear out his heart with a very sharp dagger.

Krystyn smiled as she listened to Sheila's pained screams. "It seems my beast is having fun with the little reporter. Perhaps she will die after all."

Hague swung out at the madwoman, striking her in the left breast. Krystyn yelped and grabbed her injured, and prodigious, bust.

"My tit!" she growled.

Hague saw the look on her face and knew she was going to kill him slow.

The sounds of Sheila's screams were now closer, Hague tried to pinpoint what door they were coming from. But what would it matter? He couldn't fight off the wolf-goddess, she would tear him apart with those sharp claws; maybe bite out his jugular with her fierce fangs.

A searing pain in his right arm made Rider Hague stumble to the floor--- Krystyn had landed a slashing strike that spilt his blood all over the carpet. He saw through a haze that she was going to raise her knife again and this time, he knew, the blow would be fatal.

But through the fog enveloping his vision, he thought he saw something grab Krystyn from behind, lift her off the floor and knock the knife from her hand.

Hague couldn't quite make it out, but the newcomer seemed to be incredibly large… much larger than a normal man and somewhat grotesque in appearance.

"Adam?" the professor asked as he passed out from the blood loss.

On the other side of the door that Rider Hague lay in front of, Sheila Barton found herself in a struggle for her life. The beast had torn off her gown and she now fought tooth and nail in nothing but a determined grimace. The wolf-woman had shed her own clothing as well, and now both of them fought like two fierce warriors locked in a life and death battle. But Sheila was losing, she was cut in a score of places, blood leaking from every open wound… she was getting dizzier with each passing moment. Sheila knew that sooner or later, this wolf-woman would have her way with her dead, or dying, body.

But as the beast closed in for the killing strike, the balcony doors were ripped off their hinges by someone of incredible strength.

A black-clad shape bounding into the room like a living jack-in-the-box!

Sheila knew at once who it was; the mask the shape wore giving its concealed identity away to her alone. Well, she thought, that--- and the amazing agility.

"Ravenswood!" she yelled.

The masked vampire attacked the wolf-woman with a speed unmatched. Having no place to hide or the cover of darkness to obscure her movements, Sheila noted the beast was no match for Ravenswood in a straight fight.

Both of them tumbled into the door, then right on through it!

Their battle took them out into the hallway where Sheila observed a few other familiar faces--- especially one that only she could be happy to see.

"Adam!" she cried in astonishment. "You're alive!"

Sheila wrapped a shredded sheet over her naked body and ran into the hall, glad that her monstrous savior was still alive.

But Adam was dealing with his own problems; Sheila could readily see that his skin, as well as that of the raven-haired witch with whom he fought, steamed like a neglected coffee pot on a hot stove.

"Enough," yelled Krystyn.

Strangely, all three combatants stopped fighting.

"You have all returned--- My **children**." she said, beaming. "Now my plan will be brought to fruition."

"What are you talking about?" asked Sheila. "Two of your so-called children can't even stand you."

"Ah, but that does not matter." remarked Krystyn, smiling as she walked between all of her "children". "Together the three of them are under my power; finally, they are who they were always meant be: The **Undying**."

"The 'Undying'...?"

"Yes, nosy one," spat Krystyn. "That is what they are called. What I named them.

...My triumvirate of evil. Apart they may oppose my will. But brought together I bind them to my bidding. They will serve me as long as they exist--- which is forever."

Sheila ran over to Adam and Ravenswood, grabbing both by their torn and shredded clothing.

"Come on, guys," she prodded. "Come with me."

She was trying everything in her power to make them move.

"They will not heed your call. They *answer* only to me."

"Come, my children, we must spread our reign of terror across the land. ...Across the entire planet. And then the Evil One will rise to claim this domain for all eternity."

Krystyn turned to look at Sheila, a wicked smile on her face.

"I really must thank you, my lovely," she said.

"What for..?"

"For helping me bring all my children together in one location."

Sheila felt like kicking herself, this was the army the witch had spoken of; the weapons with which she could take over the planet. And it was Sheila herself who had been the one who made it all possible for this loony bitch. Ravenswood came there to save her, and so did Adam.

Krystyn had it all planned out from the very start. Use the werewolf to cause panic, surely this would attract the attentions of a monster and a vampire... knowing that other supernatural beings were behind it all.

"But at that dive bar the other night, Adam did not recognize you. If you created him, then how could he not know you?"

"It is a by-product of the pact: if any of the three are to break off from my power... they will be cursed with a type of amnesia that can only be cured once they are *back* in my power."

"And you knew that taking me would bring both of them to you."

"When my beast told me of the masked marvel who saved you, I knew it could only be my vampire. And when Adam saved you the other night, I knew he'd be keeping an eye on you as well."

"But your werewolf kind of sunk your plans didn't she? I mean, you couldn't have known that *she'd* try to take me."

"I knew your life would be in peril and my missing children would come to your rescue. How it came to be, I did not care. The end result would be same."

"And what of Hague?" said Sheila motioning to the unmoving professor lying the floor.

"Did you kill him?"

"Mr. Hague is a wimp." Krystyn stated matter-of-factly. "He passed out from the sight of his own blood."

Sheila looked down at the prone body of Rider Hague and noted that he had a small cut on his arm, nothing serious or life threatening. She had more cuts all over her half naked body.

Sheesh, dominant member of the species, my eye, thought Sheila as she bent down to check on the "male".

"So what happens to us now?" asked the lady reporter as she smacked the wimp in his face to awaken him.

"What matter is the life of two insects when we can destroy the whole hive?"

"So, we can go?"

"I care not. You will die eventually, once my Undying wipe your kind from the face of the Earth."

"But... why? Why do you want to do this?"

"My reasons are none of your business," said Krystyn. "You're the investigator. Figure it out for yourself, but know that your time is *very* limited."

Standing before her children, the sorceress commanded them. "Come, my children, we must make way for the Evil One's return!"

Krystyn and her triumvirate of evil left the hallway and marched down the stairs. Sheila could hear them enter a room and made out the sound of a door slamming behind them.

"Come on, Hague," she said, slapping him harder.

"What?" said the dazed professor. "Am I dead?"

"Not yet, but if you don't help me, the whole human race is gonna be wiped out."

"...How?"

"That crazy witch has some kind of power over the three beings she created. We have to find some way to break that hold."

"She must be using a binding spell of some sort," said Hague, trying the clear the cobwebs.

"Yeah, she said something about binding them to her bidding."

"Then we must find a counter-spell."

"A counter-spell...? Are you joking?"

"I'm dead serious," said Hague, with some force in his voice. "If we can counter her binding spell, then maybe they'll all kill each other." "What?"

"I know you have fond thoughts for the big guy and the other one in the mask saved your life the other night, but we have no choice. Either they destroy each other or they destroy the human race."

Sheila Barton tried to contain her tears as she thought of causing the deaths of two decent beings, beings that only ever showed her kindness.

"Sheila," said Hague. "It will be better for them all. They won't be hunted no more. And they won't have to face utter loneliness every day of their lives anymore."

"I know," she said, choked up. "But they aren't evil like she is."

"Sheila… I need your help if we're to succeed. Can I count on it?"

Sheila wiped her eyes and straightened up, gazing deep in the professor's eyes.

"At least they don't glow," she said.

"Beg pardon?"

"Your eyes, at least they don't glow."

"The eyes." said Hague, trying to puzzle something out. "All of them share that same trait. Could it be of use to us?"

Sheila attempted to answer, but the question was rhetorical. Rider Hague was mumbling to himself about something.

"The fact that, all their eyes glow is fascinating," reasoned Hague. "Yes, fascinating indeed. A byproduct of the demon blood perhaps…? The one binding factor in each of them… Binding factor? That's it! The eyes are the key!"

"What are you talking about?"

Hague had almost forgotten Sheila Barton was there; her presence somewhat startling him.

"Sorry," she said.

"No problem. But I think I know how we can defeat those, what did you call them, the Undying?"

Hague spoke again before she could reply. "Yes… the Undying."

The professor smiled as he thought of something to aid them.

"But they are not, you know. They can die, just as you or me."

"So, we have to stab out of their eyes? I don't know if we can do this alone."

"No, silly, just Krystyn's… And I never said anything about stabbing them out. We merely have to destroy her hypnotic gaze, breaking her spell and in turn the pact… then the others will die as well."

"Oh, is that all?"

Rider Hague realized the sheer immenseness of such an undertaking. Even if they managed to get Krystyn alone, she was still a powerful sorceress and could probably destroy them both on her own. Then a new line of thinking began to come into the professor's head.

"There must be more demon blood around here somewhere."

"What the hell do you want that for? That's how this mess got started in the first place."

"You don't understand," he said, almost annoyed that she didn't see his intentions.

"The demon blood *is* the pact," he explained. "Once we destroy that, the witch's hold over the monsters will end, she will have failed to live up to her side of the bargain and waste away. Once their mother is gone, the monsters will shrivel up and die, or perhaps in Heidi's case, go back to being just a simple down-home girl again."

"That's brilliant, professor, but where does one keep demon blood.

"In the bookcase," he said, excited by the prospect of taking on a true high priestess, not exactly an everyday occurrence--- even for an expert in the occult.

"Which one…? She has several in that study alone."

"But we weren't in the study tonight. That dagger she stabbed me with had to have been the one she used for the sacrifices. And if she kept the sacrificial dagger in that bookcase, she would keep the demon blood there too. This is the kind of set one does not want to break up, if you catch my drift."

"One question," said Sheila. "If she used the demon blood centuries ago, why would she still have it in this day and age?"

"Probably ego," replied Hague. "Someone with an ego like that high priestess would certainly keep the one thing that could be used against her real close. And maybe she plans on creating more creatures. Who knows?"

The answer was seemingly good enough for the cute investigative reporter.

"Well, let's go kill us a thousand year old Egyptian bitch." said Sheila, exhilarated.

CHAPTER 15

Armed with a plan, Sheila and Hague headed for the parlor to search for the bookcase where they figured Krystyn would keep her sacred vial of demon blood. However, upon entering, the lady reporter felt it was a hopeless endeavor; she observed with a heavy heart that the room contained a score of bookshelves, with no doubt, thousands of books kept therein.

"I thought you said that this room only had the one bookcase." Sheila said, sarcastically.

"Well, I was deep in a trance earlier," Hague, said defensively. "I was seeing everything in a haze. Besides, you were in here too."

Sheila admitted defeat and smiled at the bookworm. He was not so bad once he was in his comfort zone, she thought.

"Where do you think the old bitch would keep the vial?" asked Sheila.

"I'm clueless, now."

"Great," said Sheila, deflated. "Now what...?"

"We only have one recourse in front of us." said Hague, thinking aloud. "We'll have to search every one of these bookshelves. Every-- last-- book."

"That could take days," Sheila stated. "Do you have any ideas in what kind of book she would keep it in? Egyptian history of something...?"

"That'd be too obvious," said Hague. "Krystyn wouldn't be so short-sighted. She is very devious, and knowing how her warped mind works... she probably hid the vial of demon blood in a book entitled 'Demon Blood'."

Sheila looked at the occult professor as if he had three heads-- she couldn't tell if he was being serious or just messing with her. After deciding that he was merely being facetious, Sheila laughed. As did he.

"So, Mr. Jokester, what do you suggest?"

"I honestly don't know."

"I do." said a familiar voice, one with a beastly tone.

Both turned to see, though knowing already, who had spoken. It was the wolf-woman!

"I see you two are hard at work," the beast snarled.

Sheila and Hague stood stock still, neither seemed sure of what to do. The beast stalked closer to them, her fangs and claws glinting in the well-lit parlor.

"You two are becoming quite annoying," she growled. "And I intend to end that annoyance."

Sheila picked up a heavy book and threw it at the she-wolf, smacking the beast squarely between the eyes, knocking her down to one knee, holding her snub-snout in pain.

"Go!" yelled Sheila, shoving the professor out of the room.

The two heroes ran toward the front door, neither one of them had a clue where to go--- but they both seemed bound and determined to "get the hell out of Dodge".

Outside of the sprawling manor, Sheila led Hague in the direction of the woods. She knew the area well enough to at least put some distance between them and the raging beast that was sure to follow.

"Where are we going?" asked Hague, short of breath.

"Jeez, prof," said Sheila. "Need to start going to gym, don't ya?"

"...Yeah." Hague puffed out in terse reply.

Sheila noticed the area to their left was flat and open, not the place they needed to go. But definitely the direction they *wanted* to go.

The lady reporter thought to herself, this is ridiculous! How the hell are we going to avoid being killed or captured by an intelligent werewolf? And what if Krystyn sent Adam and Ravenswood as well? One of them was hard enough to defeat, but three? They might as well just give up and accept their inevitable fate.

But the survivor in Sheila Barton threw that course of action out as soon as it entered her mind.

"If they want me," said the lady reporter. "They have to catch me first."

"What?" asked Hague, barely able to hear in the cool yet fierce night-wind.

"Nothing."

Sheila, recognizing a familiar path, realized with excitement it was the same one from the other night; drug the professor into the tree-thick forest ahead of them.

"I know where we are!" she crowed in excitement.

"Where…?"

But Sheila didn't answer; a sickening thought suddenly came to her--- I can't lead those creatures to Merced, only Clyde and Rich are there. And those two nice guys will not be slaughtered by my cowardly actions.

"Never mind," said Sheila. "I guess I was mistaken."

A snapping sound to the right of their location, made both stop dead in their tracks.

"I heard something." said Hague.

"Me too." replied Sheila.

Hague listened intently; now, thanks to the trees surrounding them, the wind had died down a bit, and his above-average hearing helped the professor hone in on the source.

"I think something is about fifteen yards ahead of us."

"But how could it be ahead of us?" asked Sheila, trying to figure out how the beast could've circled them in such a heavily wooded area.

"I don't know. But my sense of hearing is very acute. And I have no doubt that sound came from in front of us."

Both prepared for the attack that was sure to come their way, both unarmed and trembling from a mixture of fright and the cool mountain air.

To Hague it seemed as if hours passed before they heard any more movement and when they did, he wished it had been much longer than that.

"This is it." said Sheila, a catch in her voice.

"It was a pleasure," Hague said.

"Yeah, a real treat. We must do this again sometime."

Hague smiled at the lady reporter's brashness, even facing eminent death, the sarcasm never left her. He found he could've really fallen for this woman--- had circumstances been different.

The two held hands as they waited for the moment when they would be torn apart by needle-sharp fangs and fierce claws.

From deep in the brush, Hague saw a dark shape emerge about five feet from their position. He noted that it appeared rather short for the Undying; even Krystyn broke the five-seven mark.

"Howdy, Ms. Barton," said a man's voice, thick with a country accent. "Always in the wrong place at the wrong time, ain't ya?"

"Sheriff?" asked Sheila, relief flooding her own voice. "Oh, thank God."

"I didn't know city gals like you believed in the Almighty."

"If He saves my bacon, I believe."

The Sheriff advanced on the two haggard travelers, his flashlight illuminating their torn and ripped clothing, dirt-covered faces and scraped-up skin.

"You two been through the briars?"

"We've been running from the Undying." offered Hague.

"The 'Un-what'?" asked the Sheriff.

Hague attempted to explain, but Sheila stepped in and reminded him that one, if not all, of the Undying were in pursuit of them.

"That's right." said Hague.

"May I suggest," Sheila said. "We get out of here and hole up someplace till we can figure out a plan?"

"Come with me." said the Sheriff.

Hague was unsure, the "Sheriff" was a small guy, but Sheila grabbed his hand and pulled him along as they followed the short Sheriff out of the woods.

He knew nobody had a definite plan of action with which to proceed, yet he went anyway.

CHAPTER 16

After introducing Hague and Sheriff Monte, Sheila stepped into the Sheriff's Office; the men following her lead.

Inside the building, which consisted of the sheriff's actual office and several jail cells, the three heroes tried to come up with a feasible plan.

"What about calling in the armed services?" asked Sheila.

"No good," said Hague. "Krystyn calls these creatures the Undying for a reason. They will not die by conventional means. Only the occult can hurt them."

"I say you're wrong, young fella." Monte drawled.

"What do you mean?" asked Sheila.

"Well, from all you've told me about these Undying, seems to me they'd be susceptible to religious articles as well."

"Religion is a form of the occult," Hague pointed out.

"How's that...?" asked Sheriff Monte, obviously offended. "Come again, son, I don't think I heard you right."

"Don't get offended, Sheriff," said Hague. "I merely suggest that religion itself is based on rituality and most follow a very strict methodology. Like occult practices, religion is a common belief shared by a group of people."

"I see," said Monte, seemingly impressed.

And Sheila had to admit that she was impressed with the professor as well. He really knew a lot on the subject of the occult, or at least to her limited knowledge.

"So, we find a Catholic priest;" offered Sheila. "...Have him, what? Bless some holy water, a few crucifixes and maybe some bullets? Is that it?"

"Not quite," said Hague. "I don't think blessed bullets are the answer. I still say we need to find that demon blood and destroy it. That is the source of Krystyn's power, I'm sure of it."

"But how...? We don't know where she keeps it."

"I know." said Monte, quite sure of himself.

"This Krystyn you keep referring to--- what's she look like?" he asked.

Sheila and Hague described the raven-haired high priestess in detail. The sheriff's face immediately lit up and he stood--- not that it made much of a difference.

"Be right back," he said.

The sheriff left Sheila and Hague sitting in the office, both of them unsure of what to say to the other; so they remained silent and awaited the sheriff's return.

"Thought I'd come back and find you two sucking face." said Monte.

"Funny, Sheriff." Sheila said. "Now, why did you leave?"

"I wanted to bring someone else into our little party."

Clyde stepped into the room and Sheila immediately jumped up and hugged him.

"Shecky!" she greeted him enthusiastically.

"Hey, Missy." returned the old man. "...Nice to see you again."

"Same here."

The two parted and Clyde took a seat beside, Rider Hague. The two were introduced and then Clyde began to tell them his part in the plan.

"Well, Rich here said that you two are looking for some kind of vial ...That some dark-haired witch hid somewhere. I think I know where she might've hid it."

Sheila and Hague looked at each then at the sheriff and his cousin--- their expressions said more than anything they could verbalize.

"Couple of months back," Clyde began. "A pretty dark-haired stranger came into town, she held some kind of bag to her person as if it were some family heirloom. When I asked her if she wanted it in the safe, she nearly bit my off. She apologized and told me it was way too precious to part with. But several days later, she came to me in a huff and asked me to put her bag in the safe, urging me to not let anyone near at all… lest I pay dearly. I put the bag in the safe and there it has sat undisturbed since that day."

"Then we have an almost assured victory," said Hague, hope filling his voice. "That bag has got to contain the vial of demon blood."

As he led the three others over to the boarding house, Clyde appeared apprehensive to Sheila; his manner and being so different from what the lady reporter had come to know. Perhaps he's just excited about the prospect of taking on the forces of evil, she told herself. But the perceptive reporter in her knew it wasn't just that--- Clyde seemed almost sad?

…But why?

The monsters needed to be destroyed; even she had come to that realization. Adam and Ravenswood were beyond saving and as much as it pained her, she agreed with the professor's assessment--- their lives were full of misery and isolation. Who wouldn't choose death over that?

Sheila found herself reflecting on the last few days, something she'd felt was almost the norm now. But how could one not reflect on meeting creatures that seemingly manifested right out of the pages of fiction or from centuries of folklore?

While she took a mental pause, the lady reporter failed to notice that they'd reached the boarding house and the others had already stepped in. Sheila thought she saw something on the horizon, some kind of shape silhouetted by the full moon.

Some inhuman, beastly shape!

Sheila gulped and ran into the building, praying that Clyde had been right about the demon blood.

"There's something out there!" warned Sheila, panting.

Rider Hague recognized that the lady reporter was extremely agitated and knew at once that the Undying were indeed already in town. If this old man was wrong about the vial being still inside the safe, all their chances of survival were greatly diminished.

Not to mention the fate of everyone else on the planet.

Hague felt, for the first time, the tremendous weight that the four of them bore on their shoulders--- four ordinary, everyday human beings going up against the very embodiment of collected evil. The occult professor began to feel a bit queasy. If they failed……..

But Hague threw that thought out of his head. They had to succeed! He wanted to live so he could get to know Sheila Barton better--- maybe take her out for dinner and dancing.

"Is the demon blood still in the safe?" asked Sheila, breathlessly.

Hague noticed that Clyde was still fumbling with the combination lock, either he had forgotten the numbers or---

…Or what?

Or--- he wasn't really trying to unlock the safe.

That is ridiculous, he told himself, Clyde was the one who told them about the safe and Krystyn's mysterious bag. If he hadn't wanted to help, why would he bother alerting them to its existence?

Then it struck him! He wasn't acting out-of-character because *he* changed his mind--- someone else had done it for him--- someone with the power to control the male mind; even from long distances.

Hague sensed that Krystyn was not far from their location.

Of course! Sheila said she'd seen something outside and now the raven-haired witch was controlling poor Clyde Monte. Maybe, he thought, she controlled the sheriff as well.

"Krystyn is here." Hague whispered to Sheila. "She's taken control of the old man's mind."

"But how?" asked Sheila. "He hasn't gazed into her hypnotic stare."

Hague thought on that for a moment, she was right. Then that meant Clyde really was willingly impeding their progress.

"What's taking so long?" he asked the old man.

Clyde looked up from where he knelt by the floor safe, Hague noting that it was of basic construction: about three feet high, solid titanium alloy and anchored to the floor by four thick bolts, themselves held in place by specially added brackets.

"I don't know," said Clyde, his voice shaking.

"Calm down, Clyde," said the sheriff. "Just clear your head and try to remember the combination."

"Why can't he remember it?" asked Sheila.

Sheriff Monte leaned closer to her and Hague as he stated: "Sometimes stress can cause a temporary loss of voluntary motor function. He's so scared that his brain and hands are not coordinating properly and its taking him much longer to either remember the combination or move the tumblers to the correct position."

Hague had heard of such fright-induced "amnesia", for lack of a better word; but now was not a good time to be burdened by such an affliction.

"Got it!" Clyde proclaimed triumphantly.

The old man opened the heavy metal door with some effort and reached into the gaping maw.

"I can't seem to find the bag." he said with pronounced anxiousness.

"What do you mean?" asked Hague, perplexed.

"I mean, young fella," said Clyde, annoyed. "It doesn't seem to be here anymore."

"Great!" said Sheila, exasperated.

"Now, calm down, everybody." said Monte, ever the voice of reason. "We may have to leave and go to the next town. That idea about the religious articles may be our only chance."

"You have found your will to live on, I see." said Sheila, smiling at the short sheriff.

"Ms. Barton," he said. "I have found the need to keep you and this young fella safe. Now, let's go."

"But how are we gonna get there?" asked Sheila.

"I do have a vehicle, ya know." said the persistently cool sheriff.

"Well, then, what are we waiting for?" said Sheila, seemingly excited by the fact that all was not lost.

However, Rider Hague did not have that same optimistic outlook. Everything was such a long shot; so many "what ifs".

What if they couldn't make it to the car? What if it didn't start? What if it broke down before they could reach the next town? What if the next town was deserted as well? And what if--- they didn't have an ordained priest to bless the articles?

Hague thought about all these what ifs in less than a second, but it had been enough time for the others to head for a room in the back of the boarding house.

"Where are we going?" asked Hague.

"These buildings were constructed back in the days of the Revolution." Clyde stated. "And during construction, the builders, who had no love for the Red Coats, conspired with the architects to interconnect each one by a long "pipeline" that allowed them to sneak rebels into the town without any outside knowledge."

"Sort of like the Underground Railroad during the Civil War." Sheila said.

"I suppose." Clyde shrugged.

"But the support that the rebels got from the secret conspirators was invaluable to their cause. That's actually how this town came to be called 'Merced'. One of the revolutionaries had spent some time with the Spanish and learned some of their dialect. He claimed it meant 'mercy' or 'merciful'. I doubt anybody bothered to check out his story. Personally, I think it was just a name the founders liked and used it. Maybe it doesn't really mean anything."

Hague laughed, how many like Clyde Monte knew the history of their town yet knew nothing of the name's origin?

"Here we are," said Sheriff Monte, as he pried a fake mantle place away from the wall.

Rider Hague felt he had stepped right into pages of some "old dark house" mystery story.

But this was **real** and he kept reminding himself that the monsters chasing them were also very real.

"Help me," said the short sheriff.

Hague and Clyde stepped forward, as did Sheila Barton. All four of them pulled the façade the rest of the way from the wall. The mantle may have been for decoration, but it had weight and Hague surmised it hadn't been moved since the days of the American Revolution.

Monte pulled his flashlight out of his pocket and shined the beacon into the pitch blackness that lay before him. Hague noted, with extreme disgust, all the cobwebs that seemed to block the long unused path.

Spiders, he thought. Yuck!

"Well, people," said the sheriff. "I guess I'll lead. Since none of you appear to have a flashlight."

"Listen," said Hague. "I think one of us should take the Undying in a direction different from our intended destination."

Sheila Barton glanced at him. "You're afraid of bugs, aren't you?

"Me?" Hague feigned ignorance. "Now what makes you think...?"

The professor didn't finish his sentence, he could see in Sheila's eyes that she was not buying any of his act.

"Can't stand them." he said finally.

"I knew it."

"But the idea of misdirection for the enemy," he said. "...Is a sound strategy."

Sheila knew that Hague was correct. Someone had to lead the Undying in another direction. Someone had to act as a moving target.

But in Sheila's mind, Rider Hague did not fit that description. She would be the better candidate; she, not Hague, knew the countryside and how to survive in the woods. He was a city boy and would no doubt be killed before he got half a mile. And if he did manage to get deep into the woods, the city boy wouldn't know the first thing about "roughing it".

Not that he'd live long enough to worry about that.

"I agree," she said. "But I should be the one who does it."

Now it was Rider Hague's turn to look shocked.

"What? Are you crazy?"

Clyde and Richard Monte both stared at the two of them bickering; and something deep inside Sheila made her realize that neither of them would let her go in Rider Hague's stead. Certainly not Hague himself.

"Fine," said the lady reporter, *very* reluctantly.

Hague didn't exactly smile, but he did give her a slight smirk.

"Well," he said, extending his hand. "It's been an experience."

Sheila smiled, at least he wasn't bold enough to try for a kiss, she thought. He'd most likely get a sock in the jaw again.

…Most likely, but not definitely.

The lady reporter took Hague's outstretched hand and shook it. Then surprisingly, gave him a quick peck on the lips. The professor was so taken off-guard that he simply stood gazing at her.

"Well, young fella," said Clyde, snapping Hague out of his stupor. "You'd better get going if you're gonna be a decoy."

"Right." he said, shaking hands with the old man and the sheriff. "It's been an honor meeting both of you."

"Same here," said Sheriff Monte.

"Likewise," said Clyde Monte.

Then Rider Hague turned away and ran back into the front lobby. Sheila Barton wondered quietly if she would ever see the egghead again.

He'd really shown more guts than she would've believed of his type.

"Now," said Sheriff Monte. "Onward we go."

With that statement, the small sheriff stepped into the tunnel, his body disappearing into the dark maw as if it had swallowed him in one vicious gulp.

Clyde motioned for Sheila to enter behind his cousin, then, he brought up the rear.

All three beginning a trek through something of which none could predict the ultimate outcome.

CHAPTER 17

Rider Hague peaked out of the shuttered lobby window, noticing for the first time, that the boarding house was sparsely decorated; he figured that since the Montes were the only inhabitants, décor was probably not paramount on their list of necessities.

Hague scanned the entire area within eyeshot, seeing nothing. But, he reminded himself, that didn't mean no *thing* was out there. He swallowed hard and moved to the door, placing his sweaty palms on the brass knob. As he turned the newly-moist door knob, Hague heard a slight movement outside--- just off to the left of the other side of the mull post. Stopping just under the jamb, he took in a deep gulp of air and held his breath, lest the exhalation of give away his presence.

Now what, he asked himself. If the Undying are outside of the door, they will soon be inside and then--- then---

He didn't want to think about *what* would happen then.

Hague trying screwing up his courage, charging himself up like a biker revs up his "chopper", allowing for a quick burst of energy that would urge him to open the door, propelling himself like a bullet from a gun, run through that hidden waiting gauntlet, out into the street and from there--- deep into the dark, dark woods.

Feeling sufficiently pumped, the professor pulled the door open, swinging it back in such a forceful manner, one of the creatures actually stopped advancing and watched in seeming awe as he lunged past, jumping from the small set of steps, (three in number) and landed on the street with a soft thud. Hague wasted no time in taking off in the direction of the woods, listening as he hoofed it to the heavy breathing of his pursuer.

The professor saw no need to find out which one, if not all, now followed him into the woods.

He only hoped that Sheila and the Montes now had significant time to get deep into the pipeline and out of town.

The area Rider Hague ran to looked familiar, he decided he now had a slight bearing in which direction to go. But as he traveled deeper into the darkened woods, the occult professor admitted that maybe Sheila should've been the one doing this. What the hell did he know about surviving in the wilderness? He didn't know an oak from a fir. To him, trees were trees. His expertise was in the otherworldly--- he couldn't tell one plant from another. Couldn't direct himself by the position of the stars or the apex of the moon. Damn it! Why had he agreed to be the decoy?

Because I hate spiders, he told himself, that's why.

Spiders? Really? How about getting sliced or torn apart by some monster? Was that really a better prospect?

Funnily enough, in Rider Hague's mind--- it was.

But the occultist professor knew there was more to it; he genuinely wanted to make sure that his sacrifice would at least give the human race some time to mobilize against the Undying.

"Mr. Hague," said a voice he knew too damned well. "Why do you resist the inevitable?"

Krystyn stepped out of the shadows, flanked by her monstrous Undying children.

"We have a plan in action to stop you." he said defiantly.

"Do tell," scoffed Krystyn.

"You'll find out soon enough."

"I can make you talk." she said, matter-of-factly. "Heidi can slice into you. Adam can tear you apart. And he…" The witch ended her sentence by glancing over at the masked vampire, whose mouth was now visible under a section of torn-away cloth, a mouth full of razor-sharp fangs! The high priestess simply smiled.

"Well, you get the picture." she smirked.

"Torture me all you want," he said. "I won't talk."

"I beg to differ," said Krystyn. "Heidi…"

The wolf-goddess strode forward, her talons glittering in the pale moonlight, matched only by the horrid gleaming of her bestial yellow eyes.

Rider Hague prepared for the worst, and when the beast struck--- he screamed high into the heavens.

A scream, he felt, that seemed to echo throughout the entire forest.

In the dilapidated pipeline, Sheila and the Montes slowly made their way through what seemed like a mile of spider webs. Each had been bitten at least once as they traveled the length of the secret passage.

"Maybe the young fella was right," said Clyde. "Damned spiders are everywhere."

"We can't worry about that now," said the sheriff. "Just keep moving. The more we move, the more they scurry away."

"So you say." quipped Sheila, slapping yet another eight-legged vampire from her shoulder.

"Damn things are worse than a *thousand* Draculas." she said.

Sheriff Monte continued to lead the way through the long-unused passageway; his flashlight illuminating barely three feet of the area in front of him.

"I think we're coming to the end of the line." he said, swiping a spider from his sleeved arm.

"Thank God." said Clyde.

The sheriff shined his light on a brick wall; the mortar, to Sheila's delight, looked to be over a few hundred years old and indeed gave way as soon as the short lawman pushed against it. Sheila and Clyde both stepped forward and lent him a hand in making an escape route. Finally, they opened a hole big enough for all of them to fit, one at a time, but even the tallest of them, Clyde, could get out of it by wriggling through.

Soon, all three had emerged from the secret passage alive; dirt, dust, and spider-bite covered--- but alive nevertheless. Sheila wondered how Rider Hague was making out acting as live bait for the Undying.

For the first time upon entering the connecting room, the lady reporter noticed they had come out in one of the jail cells. And the iron bars were closed as tight as a vice.

"Now how do we get out?" she asked.

"Missy," said Sheriff Monte. "I'm the sheriff. I have the keys on my belt."

Sheila felt like an idiot, but with everything weighing on her mind, she decided that anybody could've made the same mistake. Afterall, she was only human.

"Where to now?" she asked, as Monte unlocked the cell door.

"My car," he said, sifting through the myriad of keys in his ring.

The lady reporter liked the way Richard Monte had maintained his composure through everything. She reasoned that it probably had something to do with his law enforcement training or perhaps, he became a lawman because he was just naturally a cool-under-pressure kind of person.

Whatever the reason, Sheila was glad to have him as an ally in this unearthly war. And she also liked the fact that Clyde Monte was there too. She had grown a real affection to him; that could only be described as "daughterly".

Her own father was a bit cold around the heart. When he was living, she added.

Mom was okay, but even she didn't seem as maternal as others Sheila had met.

But being here with these two amazing men in such a dire situation gave her hope for humanity, it was a small hope--- but it was hope all the same.

"Through here," said the sheriff, opening an iron door that led to the outside.

As Sheila Barton stepped out of the jail, she experienced a feeling of euphoria. The sight of the sheriff's patrol car, visible under the strong glow of a wall-mounted outside spotlight, made her smile in a way she never knew possible.

"There it is," she said, beaming.

"Yep." came Monte's only reply.

"Ever the chatterbox," Clyde joked as the three of them headed for the car: a late model Crown Victoria, the seemingly top choice for most law enforcement vehicles.

The sheriff let Sheila get in first, watching the lady reporter settle into the passenger seat, then had his cousin slip in the backseat. Sheila noted that it had no screen to keep prisoners at bay.

Monte walked around to the driver's side and stopped. Immediately, his hand went to his hip, grasping the handle of his revolver.

"I think they're here," he said through the open window, just slightly leaning down; at the same time, removing his weapon from its holster.

"Get in." said Sheila, urging him on.

"No time," he said. "Get in the driver's seat and take off. I'll do what I can to slow them down."

"No!" objected Sheila.

"Missy," he said, using Clyde's nickname for her. "If you don't leave now then no one will be around long enough for me to care."

"But," she began to protest, although she could find no valid argument to countermand his statement.

"Rich," said Clyde, leaving a simple look between the two to say it all.

"You too, Clyde…." said the Sheriff, his voice breaking. "Now git!"

Sheila Barton put the car in gear and pulled away from the brave, and soon-to-be-dead, sheriff.

The last thing she saw in the rearview, outlined by the combination of the spotlight and the car's taillights, was Sheriff

Richard Monte shooting something, then that same something pouncing on him and from there, she didn't want to know the rest.

"Damned fool," said Clyde, eyes full of tears.

"I know," Sheila consoled him, well as best as she could without being near enough to him.

"Two down and two to go," Sheila whispered to herself.

Two brave men who knew they stood no chance in hell of stopping the Undying, but tried anyway.

To Sheila, that was the true mark of a person's bravery.

Sheila Barton had no intention of letting anything happen to Clyde, he wouldn't be sacrificing his life for her. But she would gladly sacrifice hers for him.

As the lady reporter gunned the engine in the Crown Vic she was now forced to be driving, Clyde Monte shouted something.

"Look!" he screamed.

Sheila peered into the side-view mirror, and with amazement filling her eyes, she observed a pick-up truck bearing down on them at incredible speed!

"You've gotta be shitting me!" she said.

But her eyes were not deceiving her, the Undying were in the pick-up. She could barely make out their shapes in light of an oncoming dawn, yet there could be no doubt in her mind who their pursuers were.

"You'd better step on, Missy." said Clyde, urging her on.

"I've got it to the floor now."

"Which one of them do you suppose is driving?" asked the old man.

"Does it really matter?" she snapped. "We're dead if they catch up."

As Sheila gunned it, she caught sight of road sign on the shoulder of the deserted highway:

NETTSBERG
3 MILES

"The next town is about three miles or so away." said Clyde, needlessly. "You think you can stay ahead of them till then?"

"I don't know." she said, pressing the accelerator as hard to the floor as she could.

"Then we need to do something," he said.

"Like what?"

"Hand me Rich's riot gun!" said Clyde.

"Shooting them won't stop them. They can't be killed! They're immortal!"

"I'm betting that truck they're riding in isn't immune to a shotgun blast!"

Sheila grabbed the riot gun, removing the weapon from its dashboard-mounted cradle and passed it back to Clyde. He took the shotgun by its heavy stock and brought up to his shoulder. Then moving incredibly fast for a man of his age, he leaned out of the backseat driver's side window, leveling the weapon as best as he could in the fast-moving cramped space and pressed his finger to the trigger.

The blast created a spray of shot that cratered the entire front of the pursuing truck's grill and hood! "I think I might've hit their radiator with that shot!" he giggled.

"Good job, Shecky!"

But Sheila lost her smile as she noticed the truck was still advancing, slower than before, but definitely still advancing.

"They're still coming," she said.

"Shit!" yelled Clyde.

Again he leaned out and took aim, but this time, the door gave way and the old man went tumbling out of the speeding car, hitting the pavement like a discarded beer bottle! …His brittle bones shattering upon impact with the unforgiving blacktop.

Sheila screamed as she watched him lay unmoving as the pick-up neared his prone body. The lady reporter dropped her eyes from the rearview as the advancing vehicle ran over Clyde Monte's corpse.

"No, no, no! Dammit no!" she cried.

Now she was alone. No one else to help, it was just her against the Undying.

Well, if that's the way they wanna play it, she said to herself.

Sheila increased the pressure on the accelerator, making the Crown Vic go faster than she believed it could.

The writing on a new road sign cleared up as she continued down the winding highway. It read:

NETTSBERG
NEXT RIGHT

The lady reporter's heart jumped for joy as she pushed the Crown Vic to go even faster.

Nettsberg had to have a church and that church had to have a priest. The Undying didn't know it, but their evil days were numbered.

CHAPTER 18

The town of Nettsberg was not unlike Merced, the main difference being that it wasn't deserted.

Sheila sped through the town, searching on both sides of the street for a church. A town this size had to have a church, she told herself.

But she'd traveled nearly the length of the entire town and saw no cross-adorned chapel; which in her mind, was a clear indicator of a Catholic church. She began to scream in frustration, the Crown Vic wouldn't make it to another town! She had pushed the vehicle too hard for too long.

However, just as it seemed she was out of luck, Sheila Barton spied a barely visible cross over a copse of trees.

Bingo! she thought.

A church! A blessed, God-Blessed church!

As an agnostic, she had never been so happy to see a cross in her life. Spinning the car around, the harried reporter headed in the direction of the chapel.

Sheila stopped the Crown Vic in front of the church; not bothering to notice the name engraved on its wooden placard, and ran inside.

The vestibule and the nave were completely devoid of people. Sheila knew little about church practices and only knew the different parts of a church because she had researched a story about a haunted monastery in San Francisco.

Strange one, that story, seemed that in the 1600s, a defrocked priest had…

There goes the reporter taking over again, she thought, no time to think about past stories. Focus on the present or there would be no future.

"How may I help you?" asked a priest as he entered, the chancel, she believed they called it.

"I need some holy items." she said succinctly.

"Well, just about every dealer in religious miscellanea can help you there."

"You don't understand," Sheila urged. "They have to be blessed …Blessed by a priest …By someone like you!"

"What's the matter?" asked the priest.

"If I told you, you wouldn't believe me."

"Try me," he said, motioning for her sit down in one of the pews.

Sheila sat down, as did the priest, and before he could ask, the lady reporter went into a verbal rant, telling him about who she was, what she was doing there, about the Undying and most of all about Rider Hague's plan.

After she told the priest everything, she waited for his response.

"I see," he said finally. "And these creatures can only be killed by Catholic relics?"

"I suppose any religion would do." she stated. "But I don't have time to test that theory."

"Young lady," he said, rising. "If these things you need, then these things you shall have."

"Oh, thank you." she said, taking his hand.

"No, thank God," he corrected, then disappeared into a room behind the altar. Sheila also knew the name of that room, but it escaped her at the moment.

The priest returned holding several crucifixes, and a few vials she could only surmise to possibly contain holy water. He also handed her some kind of strange white garment and arraignment of bright color.

"This is a surplice and this is a stole." he said, describing the long white garment and the arraignment, respectively. "They are worn by priests while they act in Christ's stead, during the handing out of the sacraments and the reading of the liturgy."

"I have no idea what any of that means." she said as politely as possible.

"Not Catholic, huh?" asked the priest.

"Does that matter?" Sheila inquired.

"Well, faith does play a strong part in any religion--- even pagan. If you don't believe in the power within the Sacramental, if you have no faith in the sanctity of the object you're wielding to ward off evil--- then you might as well use those car keys of yours."

Sheila realized that the priest had a point; she had no faith in anything, Christian or pagan. How could she use something *she* didn't believe in?

She couldn't.

But the priest could.

"What about you, Father?" she asked. "Would your faith lend strength to these sacraments?"

"My faith?" asked the priest, somewhat caught off-guard by the comment.

"Yes, your faith. Would it be powerful enough to destroy the Undying?"

The priest sat back down and looked at the floor for a long minute, saying nothing. When he did raise his head, his eyes seemed to have gained a fire behind them that Sheila could not think possible in a man of the cloth.

"My child," he said. "I will help you vanquish these vile beasts. Every priest, or Man of God, awaits a 'Day of Trial'. And it looks as if my Day of Trial is before me. So, I must not falter in my faith, lest the Evil One and his minions take this world for their own."

Sheila glanced over some of the painted windows lining the spacious nave, she noted that each had some kind of religious significance, but didn't know for the life of her what any of them meant.

The lady reporter wanted to ask the priest, yet knew that now was not the time to be satisfying her inherent curiosity. If they lived past this day, she would ask the priest then.

If----

The priest had been in the Sacristy, as he called it, for over ten minutes. Sheila wondered what the Man of God could be doing in there so long.

Gathering his strength maybe? she asked herself.

When the priest emerged from the Sacristy, he wore a surplice, overlain with a bright-colored stole, which itself was partially hidden by a crucifix of substantial size; he also held a large book in his hand, which she figured to be a bible.

"The Rituale Romanum," he said, as he saw the question in her eyes. "It will aid us in our fight against the Evil One."

"Father," said Sheila. "May I know your name?"

"It's Alec," he said, smiling.

"I mean your first name," she corrected.

"That is my first name."

Father Alec walked away from the lady reporter looking like some kind of sacred warrior; a soldier of Christ, she supposed. At least with a priest on her side, their chances of survival increased ever so slightly. Sheila still didn't think they could beat the Undying, but what did she know? She was a reporter, an *investigative* reporter; she only things she believed in were what she could prove, what the facts laid before her could prove.

But, she told herself, if these monsters could exist--- then maybe there really was a God.

Or--- at the very least--- a Supreme Being of unlimited good of some sort.

But again, what did she know?

Sheila realized that the day was almost over and night would be falling once more. The damage Clyde inflicted to their truck must've really slowed them down. Or, maybe they had to hide during the day. She wondered where, once they arrived, the Undying would strike. Would they come straight for her, or just begin their reign of terror on the first poor soul who happened to cross the path of their cold, gleaming eyes?

The lady reporter shuddered when she imagined what they'd done to Rider Hague and Richard Monte. She was sure neither of their deaths had been quick or merciful.

Sheila nearly threw up as a vision entered her mind of them both being tortured endlessly.

Hopefully, they died quickly, she thought. Please, God, if you exist, let that have been the case.

"Sheila," said Father Alec. "It's time."

"What do I do?" she asked.

"Well, since you have no faith in the sacred power these objects possess," he stated. "I guess, you could learn a quick prayer that might help you if I am to fail in my mission."

"If you fail, Father, we're all dead."

"Not so," said the priest. "There are many believers in the One God. They may not all be Catholic, but they do believe in an Omnipotent Creator. The Almighty, if you will."

"I wish I had your faith, Father."

"Alec," he said.

"Father Alec," she corrected herself.

"No, just Alec," said the priest with a warm smile.

"Is it true priests don't…" Sheila couldn't finish the question.

"What?"

"Well… anything. They don't drink, smoke, have sex. They don't seem to be allowed to have any fun in life."

"Sheila, I was a teenager just like you. Just like most people. And just like most people, I did plenty of everything before I got the 'Call'."

"The Call?" asked Sheila, unsure of its meaning.

Too late to stop now, she told herself, and kept running. Within seconds, she reached the spot where she had seen the bag fall. But unfortunately, it no longer seemed to be there.

Quickly, Sheila dropped to one knee and scanned beneath the Crown Vic. Sure enough, right in the middle of the vehicle's undercarriage, just out of reach, lay the bag.

Why is it never easy? she asked no one in particular. Or maybe she was addressing a God she didn't believe in. Sheila quickly started to crawl underneath the car, reaching for the one item that could possibly save all of humanity.

As she scooted further under the vehicle, Sheila felt something grab her ankle and begin dragging her back out. The lady reporter kicked at the thing holding her, trying to make it release, or at the very least, lessen its grip. Suddenly, the hand let go and Sheila heard whatever it was scream as if being tortured. She guessed that Father Alec had thrown some more of that holy water stuff at one of the Undying.

Damned good stuff, that.

Finally, Sheila got hold of the bag and opened it. She couldn't quite make out its contents, but as she felt the outside, the lady reporter could discern the shape of something inside; something that could've been a glass vial. Reaching her hand into bag, Sheila rummaged through a gaggle of items. One of the things she touched felt slimy and sticky, she didn't want to know what it was, so she kept searching for that damned demon blood!

Outside of her vehicular sanctuary, Sheila heard the sounds of a pitched battle; then shuddered involuntarily as she heard a scream that sounded too human to be one of the monsters.

Oh, no, she thought, Father Alec.

The priest's limp body fell onto the sidewalk, his bloody hand hanging over the curb beside which the Crown Vic was parked. The lady reporter suppressed a yell and just stayed focused at the task at hand.

To her utter amazement, the Crown Vic suddenly left the ground and she found herself unprotected and lying before the Undying with Krystyn's bag in her still outstretched hands, still trying to find the damned vial.

"You killed the priest?" she asked.

"Of course," said Krystyn, her bronze skin showing a nasty burn where the holy water had struck it. "He was merely an obstacle… such as you. And now, I intend to get rid of you once and for all."

Ravenswood grabbed Sheila by her hair, lifting the lady reporter from the ground as if she weighed nothing. His dark glasses now gone, she noticed his eyes were indeed red. Those same glowing red eyes she'd seen as a little girl. But she also now saw a mouth and nose composed of rotting flesh.

Sheila shuddered at the sight of his partially unmasked face and his blood-soaked vampire fangs.

"Ravenswood," she said, trying to make him remember her. "Please don't do this."

"He does not recognize you anymore," Krystyn gloated. "He responds only to my commands."

The semi-masked vampire carried her over to his mistress like an obedient dog bringing back a fetched stick. Sheila still struggled through the bag, her hand finally striking something that felt like a vial.

Found it! she screamed in her mind.

But it was too late, Krystyn had just ordered Ravenswood to kill her.

However, the masked vampire did not move.

"Did you hear me?" ordered Krystyn. "I said kill her."

Yet he moved not a muscle to harm her; there must've been some part of him, some hidden part of his psyche that remembered her.

Krystyn backhanded Ravenswood, making him drop Sheila on the hard pavement.

"You will pay dearly for disobeying me!"

The witch turned her attention to Adam, motioning for him to approach. Then with a bronzed hand, Krystyn ordered him to kill the lady reporter.

Sheila covered her head as he strode toward her, it wouldn't take much for him to tear her apart, limb from limb.

And yet again, the killing blow did not come.

"I said kill her!" screamed Krystyn, hysterical.

Adam didn't raise an arm against Sheila, just looked down at her with glowing green eyes.

The raven-haired witch pushed him aside and reached for Sheila herself, producing that nasty dagger she had used to cut Rider Hague and killed most likely many others throughout the centuries.

"Now, bitch," she said, lifting Sheila up. "You die by my hand."

With that proclamation, she drove the sacrificial dagger deep into Sheila's chest!

The lady reporter fell to her knees, blood spilling from the wound like a crimson waterfall.

"You will annoy me no longer." said Krystyn, triumphantly. "… So says the High Priestess of Sutah, god of the deserts."

Sheila Barton lie in the middle of the street, dying; watching her life's blood spill forth and flow onto the pavement, forming a pool around her prone body--- but she still had presence of mind to take the vial she hid in her bloody hands and smash it to the ground!

The lady reporter watched as realization, alternating with terror, filled Krystyn's beautiful face. Then she observed with great delight that the witch's beauty had started to deteriorate. And her entire body began to at first wrinkle, then, shrivel up before her own wide, frightened eyes.

Sheila smiled as she saw the shriveled body lose its integrity and finally collapse on the pavement in a pile of centuries-old dust!

She had won!

She had beaten the witch who tried to destroy all mankind.

A hard, basically faithless woman, she scoffed, had ceased the annihilation of every man, woman and child on Earth.

As she took her last breath, and life drained completely from her--- the last thing Sheila Barton ever saw in **this** Life was the Undying… dying.